THE UMBRELLA GRAVEYARD

THE UMBRELLA GRAVEYARD

Rachel Donkersley

APEX PUBLISHING LTD

First published in 2005 by
Apex Publishing Ltd
PO Box 7086, Clacton on Sea, Essex, CO15 5WN

www.apexpublishing.co.uk

Copyright © 2005 by Rachel Donkersley
The author has asserted her moral rights

British Library Cataloguing-in-Publication Data
A catalogue record for this book
is available from the British Library

ISBN 1-904444-32-6

Typeset in 11.5pt Baskerville

Cover Design Andrew Macey

Printed and bound in Great Britain

Contents

1
Start

I like to walk in the rain. That might sound a little bit strange. Most people like to watch or listen to the rain beating down outside whilst they are snug in their living rooms, warming their hands in front of the fire, or around a cup of hot chocolate.

Winter is my favourite time of the year; the colours, the smells, the excitement of Christmas. I love to be outside, the rain like background music, or in my car, music turned up, heaters on, the headlights illuminating the open road.

You might be wondering why I'm telling you all this, but you'll need to know how it started, all this...weird stuff. Well, that's how it started. With the rain.

I'd been over at my parents' house for Christmas. I had arrived on Christmas Eve, the Wednesday night, just in time for the Christmas Eve carol concert at the village church! I had stayed through until the weekend and was heading back home on the Sunday evening for the yearly inconvenience of working the few days between Christmas and New Year.

My parents live in a small village called Hepby, up in the Yorkshire Dales. Hepby is where I grew up, where I went to school, the place that I grudgingly left five years ago to take a place at university in London. I never returned to the village for good after that, but I'm working in York at the moment, putting my architectural studies into practice, so it's much easier now to visit. Hepby is a beautiful place. In summer you can see for miles, and it's all fields, sheep, dry-stone walls and the odd farmhouse.

It was always a bit of a Sunday tradition in our family to go for a walk after dinner. We must have walked for miles back in those days, and covered every inch of the village and its neighbouring landscapes. We would set off, whatever the weather, just the three of us and our dog, Cal, who I had named, aged twelve, after my dad had let me stay up one night and watch *East of Eden* with him. He then continued over time to mould my taste in films, and a conversation about James Dean or John Wayne could always be relied upon to provoke some friendly family debates. This was what I loved about going back to Hepby: the late night chats in front of a real coal fire and catching up on all the local gossip; you'd be surprised how much news a small village is capable of producing, Hepby could fuel its own soap opera! My mum, of course, loved having me back for Christmas, so that she could fatten me up and show me off to her friends. I know some of my friends would rather do anything than have to sit through a family Christmas, but it's always been different with our family, and Hepby is the perfect setting for a traditional Christmas. We even had some snow on Christmas Eve, and so woke up on Christmas morning to a view of the white-tipped hilltops. There's nowhere I would have rather been for Christmas, and nothing I hated more than having to leave halfway through the festivities to return to York.

I was brought up in the countryside and now I can only stay away for so long before I'm pining for the fresh air and an escape from the city. I still like to go for a walk around the village when I visit Hepby: it's much more relaxing and better for getting rid of stress than a session in the gym or a couple of hours in the pub. I can still stand there and look out over the countryside for hours. It's peaceful and still, and it's home.

My name is Declan Patrick Jones - the product of an Irish grandmother and a Welsh father - but everyone calls me Paddy. We've still got relatives over on the west coast of Ireland, mainly in Westport I think, although I've only been as far as Dublin and I've got a broad Yorkshire accent, but Paddy's okay with me!

So I had left my parents' house at about eight o'clock on the Sunday evening, the twenty-eighth of December. It was wet and cold outside as I drove along the familiar winding country roads. I had the radio on which was playing some sort of Christmas jazz festival and the rain was beating down on the windscreen. Now, I would normally be in a bit of a rush to get home, especially on a Sunday night, when I'm rarely organised for a Monday morning back at work. I wouldn't have any shirts ironed and all the little jobs I'd put aside for the weekend would most probably be on a mental 'To Do' list. My flatmate, Alistair, was having some friends over for the weekend, a little 'post-Christmas party' he said, so no doubt I would find myself reluctantly cleaning up after them, following the usual dilemma of not being able to find any clean cups and plates in the cupboard. So, this particular night I didn't feel in any rush to get home. I'd had such a relaxing few days off work, away from the city, and Monday morning still seemed to be such a long way away. For the time being I was enjoying the rainy drive back to York, and I was taking my time with it.

I was also maybe a little more thoughtful than normal because my grandad had been taken into hospital a week earlier, the day of my twenty-third birthday. This was following his second heart attack and his stubborn attempt to convince the doctor that he would be fine if they could just leave him alone in his own house. This trait has been unfortunately passed down through generations of the

Jones'; we don't like to be told what to do and we always know what is for the best! Little did I know then that I was on the verge of something that would test not only my strength of mind but also my already super-charged imagination. My grandad had therefore spent Christmas in the General Infirmary, which was in the next town, ten miles away, so I had spent quite a few hours during my stay either sitting with him or driving other members of my family to the hospital and back.

Although I wasn't really ready to leave, and would have liked to have stayed in Hepby a bit longer, the slow, rainy drive home provided some well-timed relief from the rush of the previous few days, and the confines of my warm car were not only protecting me from the storms but also giving me a little break from reality and a bit of time to myself. My parents' house had been bustling with relatives, friends, and lots of people I'd never met before, and in fact I'm not sure my parents had either. That's the thing about living in a small village; everyone knows everyone else, and from the day a new family moves in they treat every other house in the village like a second home. It's nice I suppose, but maybe a bit too much to put up with all of the time. My mum seems to like it though; there's always someone calling in on their way back from a shopping trip, or someone making a detour home from work just to say hello. They mustn't ever get any time to themselves. There's no such thing as a private life in Hepby, and the social scene is pretty non-existent; all the reasons I love Hepby are the same reasons I left!

Anyway, as I said I was driving back to York. I knew this route off by heart; I always drove on the back roads, opting for the quietness of the countryside and the scenic route rather than the mundane view of the motorway. It was about halfway up the steep hill that led to the main road that I

4

decided impulsively to pull over into the lay-by. I turned off the engine and stepped out of the car. The heavy rain had turned, momentarily, into a light drizzle and for a few minutes I stood next to my car looking up at the moon. It was too good to miss. The black fields, the stars lighting up the quiet, tiny village. It had once been a busy little place, when I was at school there, or maybe that's just how I remember it. Now the shops were closing one by one as people moved nearer to the towns, nearer to the schools and their jobs. There were still plenty of people around during the day time, and an extra helping of visitors at Christmas, in fact it even saw some tourists during the summer, but the businesses were struggling as young families were slowly being replaced by retired couples.

Across from the lay-by was a row of three terraced shops. There was Mrs Stevens' grocery shop on the left, our friend Jane's flower shop in the middle and old Mr Smith's DIY shop on the right. There wasn't what you might call a centre to Hepby where all the shops and local amenities were; everything was spread out. The school sat on its own at the peak of a steep hill, a relatively long walk away from the three shops opposite the lay-by, and unless you were wanting groceries, flowers or a new screwdriver set you had to walk even further to the next row of shops, which in fairness probably sold much the same. Something like this, which would eat away at my patience after a while, seemed very popular with the elderly people and the mothers that stayed at home. They enjoyed setting off in a morning with an empty basket, collecting eggs and milk from one shop, bread from the baker's a mile down the road, and bacon from Ken the butcher if he had decided to open that day. They liked it because they got some exercise, the odd neighbourly chat along the way and fresh, locally produced food. If you wanted to buy everything all together in a supermarket you had no option but to drive into the next town, which most people wouldn't dream of! I sometimes think that they liked to believe they were living in another era, a million miles away from the modern-day world.

I stood there in the drizzle for a few minutes, starting to wish I could stay there a little bit longer and wondering why the company I worked for couldn't have just closed for two weeks. I don't think I'll ever get used to working over Christmas. I preferred it at school when we got the whole fortnight off. It's no wonder Christmas is more exciting when you're a kid; it's all you've got to think about for two weeks! Anyway, thinking this irrelevant nonsense wasn't going to change the fact that I had to be in work the following morning at nine o'clock.

It was just as I was about to get back in my car that I noticed the light. At first I thought it was just a light that had been left on in the DIY shop, but then I noticed that it was getting brighter and then dimmer and appeared to be swaying from left to right across the rooftops. It was an almost blinding white light and my eyes could only just stay open long enough to take a glimpse of it. I tried to watch the light as it swung back over to the right, much brighter than the understated orange streetlights that gave the village its old-fashioned feel. I looked around to see if anyone was about, then I crossed the road to have a closer look. I knew I shouldn't really be venturing into the darkness at the back of the shops, on this deserted street, just out of curiosity. I knew anyone or anything could have been lurking there. I've watched enough horror films to have acquired quite an imagination, but I also knew that this was just Hepby, our little village, and nothing *ever* happened there. The closer I got to the light, the more I knew I wasn't going to take any notice of my common sense; I certainly couldn't just ignore it and walk back to my car.

As I got onto the path that ran down the right-hand side of the DIY shop, the light seemed to stop moving. It was even brighter now, but it was still and focused on a single point on the roof. I followed the path round to the back, where it runs between the three shops and the playing-field wall, trying to find the source of the light. I kept walking towards it as, although it was still, it seemed to be taking me somewhere, showing me the way, leading me to…my car?!

How strange! I knew the path didn't lead back onto the road. It ran all the way down to the next farmhouse. So how had I just walked round in a circle? I stood there frowning to myself for a minute and contemplated giving up on this heroic combat with a runaway light but, well, whilst I was there I thought I might as well have one more attempt. I didn't understand what was happening and that made me even more determined to find out.

I set off again, down the path to the right of the DIY shop, and making a conscious effort to concentrate I walked along the path, following the light. I could see quite clearly, even through the blinding whiteness, that the path ran in a straight line behind the back of the shops and continued all the way down to Mulberry Farm, but despite my strenuous efforts I ended up back on the main road, looking over at my car.

Feeling a little frustrated by this time, but nevertheless still very curious, I decided to try walking in the opposite direction. I took the DIY shop as my starting point as before, then I walked past the florist's, on to the grocer's and pulled myself through the narrow opening at the left of the shop. I assumed that this must have been where I detoured off the path and emerged, unintentionally, back onto the main road.

This time, as I reached the path from the other side, I realised that the light had disappeared and I was standing there in darkness as the storm began again. The rain was beating down much heavier now, making it even more difficult for me to see where I was going, and even just keep my balance. I then remembered why I had begun looking over by the shops in the first place; I was supposed to be checking that everything was okay, looking for burglars, or a late-night group of delinquent school kids. However, now I was a bit scared. I wasn't feeling quite so brave any more without the comfort of the street being conveniently lit up for me. I made my way down the path, stumbling along as quickly as I possibly could. At last the path came to an end, and there I was, back on the main road, yet again standing outside the DIY shop, although this time feeling quite relieved that I had survived the ordeal in the dark. But I was obviously mistaken about the path. Things really had changed since I'd been away!

I walked across to the lay-by, absolutely soaking wet, ready by this time to get back in my car and resume my journey home. It was then that the whole sky opened up. The storm became silent and the rain stopped. The streetlights went out and the entire village was illuminated by hundreds of bright white lights, swaying across the rooftops like the one I'd just seen. It was brighter than daytime, and although there still wasn't anyone around I could hear bells ringing and music coming from somewhere. As I turned to look behind me, I saw that the fields were no longer black, but lit up with a working fairground. The children's rides were spinning around, the horses on the roundabout were nodding their heads, the ghost train was screaming, the chair-swings were flying, but there was not a single person in sight. I looked back towards the shops. Yes, the lights were on but there definitely wasn't anyone home.

This was my chance, I decided, to have one last look around the back of the shops, and solve the mystery of the runaway path. So I set off again, to the DIY shop, round the back and onto the path. There was the light again. Amongst all the other lights that had just been switched on, this one light swaying across the rooftops of the three tiny village shops was still the brightest, and now I could see where it was coming from. This time, instead of giving in and following the beam back onto the road, I followed it the other way, hunting out whatever it was that was creating this blinding light. As the beam narrowed, the light became even brighter and the newly lit-up village slowly faded into the background. As I reached what I thought must be the source of the light, by now I was over the wall and lost in the midst of the playing field, the sky opened up again, this time taking with it all the lights, the fairground and the sun and leaving me, for the second time that evening, standing in the dark, under an angry, thunderous storm.

2
Inside the Safe

Catching glimpses of my new territory by the flashes of lightning falling to the ground, I set off in an attempt to find cover from the torrential rain. The playing field had become almost unrecognisable in the darkness and so I just had to continue walking across the wet muddy ground, completely blind to my surroundings, hoping that eventually I would bump into something.

I obviously knew that there was a playing field behind the shops, in fact I think we played football on it sometimes back in junior school, but as far as I knew it didn't lead anywhere in particular. I suppose I assumed it just backed onto more fields; everywhere did in Hepby. Something didn't feel right though, and I know it's easy for me to say that now, looking back on it, but I knew that the playing field couldn't have been so big that you wouldn't have been able to see the main road from it, or the shops, or Mulberry Farm. So it was at that point that I started to think I might have ventured a little further than I had first thought. If I stood in any one spot and spun round I saw only darkness, nothing else at all, and if I had been in that playing field I would surely have been able to make out the streetlights on the main road, or even the odd light on up in the hills.

It's a funny feeling to be in pitch blackness because you are completely disoriented and, as you can imagine, this added to the confusion that had already been created by my detour, so I was completely unable to make a decision as to which way to start walking. How could one direction be a better choice than the next? So I continued to wander aimlessly and waited patiently for each strike of lightning because, as frighteningly loud as the roll of thunder that preceded it was, it was my only aid for seeing in the dark.

Piecing together the snapshots as I looked around, I realised that I was soon standing in front of a massive house. It looked like an old suburban American-style house, with painted white shutters on the windows, a white garden fence and a porch with a swing. The porch became my saviour as I stepped up onto it out of the horrific weather. I couldn't see further than the fence in front of me so I was unable to work out whether it was a street I had stumbled across, full of these old houses, or whether it was just an unusual kind of old farmhouse that somehow I hadn't noticed before. From what I could make out in the distance and the general atmosphere that seemed to have been created around me, it still didn't feel familiar to me as most of Hepby does, but at the same time I kept thinking...I couldn't have walked that far could I? I was sure even by walking slightly too far across the playing field I couldn't have come across another village, or even just another street; everywhere else was miles from Hepby and I knew the location of every street off by heart. I had no idea how far I was from the safety of the main road and I was starting to wish that I'd ended up by my car again so I could escape this confusion.

I jumped out of my skin when the front door opened. A light had been on inside the house the whole time I had been standing there. Why hadn't I noticed that before? Now I realised that I was standing at a stranger's front door, dripping wet and lost! And it was all due to my insatiable curiosity that I had ended up there. How was I going to explain this one?

I needn't have worried as a very kind-looking woman, I'd

say probably in her early seventies, appeared at the door with a smile. She was wearing a pale blue dress and white apron and her silver hair was partially covered by a red headscarf.

'Come on in dear, out of the cold,' she greeted me kindly through the screen door.

I was certain that I didn't know her from the village. Maybe she knew me as a child and expected me to remember her? That seems to happen quite a lot to me when I go home to Hepby after being away for a while.

Anyway, I didn't really have much choice; it was either fighting the elements in an attempt to find my way back to my car, or it was sheltering indoors until the storm calmed down, so I took up the woman's offer and stepped inside out of the cold. The kitchen was immediately inside the front door, and the only room of the house that I saw. There was a door leading out of the kitchen, but that was kept firmly closed, and I noticed clothes drying on a clothes-horse and a big old sofa with a patchwork quilt draped over it. It looked like the woman could just have been living in that one room. The entire kitchen, however, was immaculately clean; it was blue and white, matching the woman's clothes, and, with a pristine Aga in the corner, it was of the same era as the exterior of the house. I sat down on one of the benches at the large wooden table as the woman turned off the stove, lifted off a saucepan of boiling milk and poured it into two cups of powdered cocoa. It was almost like she had been expecting me.

She joined me at the table and we spoke briefly about the storms outside before she asked, 'So what can I do for you?'

I looked up at her, slightly shocked, and frowning because I had absolutely no idea what I was doing there. I didn't want to appear ungrateful, though, for the cup of cocoa and the shelter from the rain, so like a lost child who can't find his way home I attempted a smile and hoped she'd be able to help me.

'I'm sorry,' I said. 'I don't actually know where I am. If I know you I'm sorry I don't remember you.'

'Oh no dear, you don't know me,' the old woman laughed. 'I'm Mrs Featherstone, and you are...?'

'Paddy.'

'Nice to meet you Paddy.'

We both took a few sips of the hot cocoa, and then she continued.

'Let's make this a little easier shall we? No, you don't know me but I'm very pleased to have met you. You don't know where you are, but I do. You don't know why you are here, but I do. You don't know where you're going. You don't know whether to be afraid or not. You won't know who anyone is around here, yet you think you've lived here all your life. So, let's rephrase the question. Is there anything you want to ask me?'

We sat in silence as Mrs Featherstone and I both waited for a question to pop into my head. What did I want to know? All of these things? Or none of them?

'Okay,' I said deciding to play along. 'Where am I and how do I get back to my car?'

'Are you in a rush, dear?'

'Well, it's just that I was on my way home. I've got work tomorrow. I wasn't exactly planning on taking this detour. I think I might have got a bit lost. Things seem different around here.'

'Well, that's because you haven't been here before. We've always been here, but you've never visited us up until now. You think this is Hepby, a part of the village that you have somehow overlooked, but it isn't. This dear, is Tunnelton, and we're a long, long way away from your car.' She laughed as she spoke, but it was a soft and kind laugh. She wasn't laughing at me, she was just happy!

I was confused, obviously. I'd never heard of Tunnelton. How could I have come across it, driving as normal along the familiar roads of Hepby? Without my speaking this question out loud, Mrs Featherstone answered me.

'You cracked the code, dear,' she nodded. 'That's how you got in.'

I frowned yet again and shook my head to indicate that I still didn't understand.

'You walked around the shops. Twice anticlockwise, and then once clockwise. You waited for the light to return and then you followed it into the playing field. It's a human safe, dear, and here you are!'

Noticing my astonishment, Mrs Featherstone stood up and patted my shoulder, and as she walked out of the kitchen into the great unknown of the house said,

'Stay here until the rain stops, dear, and then go and have a walk around outside. You'll understand.'

3
Daylight-Saving

The first thing I noticed as I stepped outside a couple of hours later was that this whole village, this hidden town, had no particular order to it. It couldn't be defined. The house I'd just left could have come straight out of fifties America, but the road it was on wasn't from any specific era. The house to the left, although it was a good distance away, was modelled on the Temple of Artemis, partially constructed of marble and with impressive columns, although probably slightly shorter than the original, on display housing the front door. The house to the right was a miniature medieval castle with tiny square windows and the family crest painted on the oversized wooden door.

The whole place was a patchwork of decades, of films and influences; a hybrid of black and white and colour, of people and animals, of town and country, of sun and rain, light and dark, night and day. It was fascinating and beautiful, yet indisputably dream-like.

Now, although I quite often catch myself deep in thought, trying to find explanations for some of life's great mysteries, I still like to think of myself as pretty down-to-earth. I've got my head screwed on. I try to think rationally, control my temper, avoid being caught up in all this day dreaming, and I can be a little sceptical sometimes, but this...this dream I wanted to be a part of.

The second thing I noticed was that it was light. My logic told me that it must have been quite late by this time so why was the sun still out? I looked at my watch, but that didn't

15

help as it seemed to have gained a mind of its own; it was stopping and starting randomly. I made a mental note to get it fixed.

I wandered a little farther afield, away from the relative comfort of Mrs Featherstone's warm kitchen and onto the nearest path. The street that the houses were on was just a trodden dirt path that connected them together. It could quite easily have been part of Hepby's playing field, although I knew for certain now that it couldn't be. The main country roads wound themselves in and around the fields, separated by low walls and thick hedges. It reminded me very much of our village of Hepby. The sheep and cows grazed happily across the acres of farmland and as I took a walk along the narrow winding roads I started to feel very much at home. I chose a direction at random as from this point I couldn't see very much at all other than fields, and so I began walking up a hill that I came across, thinking that if I got a bit higher up it might help to realign my senses if I could see where I was and where I was going!

I didn't bump into anyone for what felt like hours, by which time I was lost in thought, marching steadily up the hill, but then out of the corner of my eye I noticed a woman with a pushchair walking down the hill towards me. She stopped when she saw me and crossed over the road.

The woman reached out to shake my hand and she introduced herself as Stephanie. I wondered if she too was going to give the impression that she knew me, but she didn't mention anything so I told her my name and when she asked me where I was walking to I answered honestly and told her that I was just trying to find my way around. We began talking about the town; or rather she talked about the town whilst I tried to pretend I knew where I was and what I was doing there.

16

'There's a good view from the top if you make it that far' Stephanie said.

From where we were now I could just about make out some buildings down in the valley, but was still unsure as to how I might get down there. They just seemed to collect at a centre-point where the fields ended and some sort of civilisation began.

'I'll do my best,' I said as I looked up ahead trying to gauge how far the 'top' might be.

The child was asleep in the pushchair and we were both taking a rest as we spoke by leaning, half-sitting, half-standing, against the wall. All of a sudden it went dark. I looked up to the sky. It was just like night-time, which I supposed it must be; I'd just never seen it arrive at such speed. The sky was black, the stars were out and the streetlights, although there weren't any down the country lane where we were standing, were all on further down in the village. My face shone with disbelief again. What was happening?

'It's okay,' Stephanie reassured me. 'I can tell you're not from round here.' She pointed up at the sky, 'It's just Daylight-Saving.'

Having given up on trying to appear informed about these strange Tunnelton happenings, I asked,

'Daylight-Saving? Isn't that just when we put the clocks back an hour?'

'That's what Daylight-Saving means to you, yes, but here things are a little bit different. Daylight-Saving is literally saving daylight. There aren't a lot of people around at the moment. No cars on the road. Most people will be in bed or at work depending on their shift pattern, and we're standing still, so the sky just closes up. Once you start walking back up this hill it will appear to be day time again, lighting up the road for you to see where you're going.'

I stared up at the night sky and wondered whether I was going to understand anything in this town.

'Don't think about it too much,' Stephanie continued. 'Or think of it like saving energy, because it's no different. For example, if you're not using a room, you switch the light off don't you? If you don't need it, why waste it? This works on the same principle. Everything runs on solar power here. Every house, building, car and train contains its own little power station: solar panels and battery packs from which everything runs. We're very economical here you know!'

I nodded back at her, and said she was probably right the first time, I shouldn't think too hard about it! We said goodbye as I set off again up the hill, daylight returning as if at the flick of a switch!

4
Deer Mountain

I must have fallen asleep after my long walk up the hill because I woke up on a park bench under a big oak tree with the morning sun beating down on me. I knew I must have been walking for miles. I'd just kept on going, thinking that as long as the sun stayed out for me I might as well try to get as far as I could. I thought that the higher up I got, the easier it would be to make out the shape and size of the town and plan my route into the town centre, where I thought it was more likely I might recognise something or someone, or at least find a way to escape!

I looked down over the hillside to see the lights and movement of the town centre. Well, I was still only assuming it was the town centre. It appeared to be the core of this town, if in fact it could be described as a town. I hadn't ventured far enough by this point to know how big the place was. Mrs Featherstone had told me that things would start to make sense when I came to have a look around outside, but so far my experiences had only succeeded in confusing me even more. My conversation with Stephanie had, at least, filled me in about the unusual activities of the sunlight, but brought another thousand questions to my mind at the same time. If something as basic to life as sunlight could confuse me, how likely was I to understand anything about my new surroundings?

All I knew for certain at that particular moment was that I was very high up. I had walked a fair distance up the hill and from my position on the bench I could look down over the fields and valleys, but I could still only just see the peak of the hill that I had been climbing. I hadn't even reached the top yet!

I was feeling hungry by this time and very thirsty from the long walk the night before. There appeared to be a café a little higher up, right at the top of the hill, so I got myself up and carried on walking.

The top of the hill really was the highest point of the town and looking down over the other side I could see groups of people hiking up what from this angle was definitely a mountain. I really must have been walking for hours, but I was just slowly pacing up country roads. The mountain side was a steep, rubbly climb. Why didn't all these people come up the other way the same as I did? Surely that was a quicker and less tiring way to get to the top.

Too sleepy to think at that moment I headed for the café. At the top of the mountain side there was a carved wooden sign planted in the ground that read 'Congratulations! You have climbed Deer Mountain!' and the sign above the café said 'Deer Mountain Café'. What was this place and why was it so popular? I went inside and ordered a cup of tea and a full cooked breakfast. That would keep my energy up for a bit more exploring!

I sat there for a while trying to gather my thoughts, trying to come up with some sort of plan as to how I was going to get myself out of there. Although I knew I was in a strange place, a place that couldn't possibly really exist, it just felt like I was on holiday, finding my way around and getting to know my new environment. There was nothing scary about it, nothing that set the alarm bells off in my head. It was a pleasant, friendly place. I had some money with me, and warm clothes on, although I would soon find out when I attempted to pay for my breakfast how little use money would be to me on this trip. The café owner just smiled at me as he handed over my plate of bacon and eggs.

'Put your money away son, it's no use here' he said.

Although I knew at the back of my mind that I should be making some attempt to get home, I had to admit that I had quite enjoyed my first few hours there'.

I came to the conclusion, on a full stomach, that the best thing to do would be to make my way down the mountain, follow the lights to the centre of the town, and then find someone who would point me in the right direction home.

The peak of the mountain was - had to be - a tourist attraction. Upon leaving the café I stood for a second time at the highest point of Deer Mountain and took a good look around. It seemed quite clear to me; on one side there was a winding country road that took its time to reach the top, whilst on the other side there was a steep, rugged pathway that begged for the sweat, tears and perseverance that befitted a hike up a mountain. There were plenty of people around, people just like me. Whether they were inhabitants of my 'Newfoundland', or whether they were visitors, lost or otherwise, educated in this piece of land's existence within our Yorkshire countryside I have no idea, but they were no more friendly or unfriendly than other people I've met on my travels elsewhere. I felt as safe, intrigued and curious as I would anywhere else I hadn't visited before.

There was only one way down for me, even though it was effectively swimming against the tide, as groups of people, families young and old, trekked up the path in search of the infamous Deer Mountain Café. I sped down the mountain the only way you can descend such a steep hill forwards, by leaning back, stomach muscles clenched as my feet ran away with me.

I got about a third of the way down and took a rest on a

small diversion to the main walkway - a short platform about three feet long that hovered nervously over the edge, threatening to snap off at any moment and send me crashing to my death. The fields that surrounded the path looked very similar to the ones I had seen on the way up but it must have been a fair distance to the other side; this was a big old mountain. I saw cows and sheep and a perfect example of the art of dry-stone walling. Then it occurred to me as I took a long drink of the water I had luckily thought to get at the café, where were the deer?! I shook my head in answer to my own question. Was there a simple explanation for anything in this town?

I set off on the second part of my descent. The path itself must have been redefined at a much later date than the walls had been built because you could tell they were made out of very old stone which was crumbling in parts and was extremely well weather-worn. It was a relatively narrow path for a place expecting so many visitors, and it was covered in washed pebbles rather than dirt and grass as you might expect; tarmac would have made it easier for walking on! The tourists however, came in their groups nonetheless, the crunching sound beneath their feet and mine as we passed one another, instinctively keeping to the left.

It took me another good hour-and-a-half of walking, or, more precisely, running with the brakes on, before I could even see the bottom of the mountain, the finishing banner for this reverse hike. I needed to stop for another rest and as I slowed to a halt, panting for breath and sweltering in the heat, I finally stopped someone on their road to discovery to enquire about the name.

'Excuse me,' I asked, 'can you tell me where this mountain gets its name? It's just that I've walked up one side and down the other and I haven't seen a single deer.'

'Well of course not, son,' the man laughed. 'There aren't actually any deer. It's just a mountain with a deer tattoo. It is as old as Tunnelton itself, a natural creation in the land structure that has since been defined by the stone walls to make it easier to see and enjoy.'

'A deer what? Tattoo?' I asked again.

The man, a greying, bespectacled man in his late fifties with a horde of children and grandchildren, turned me round, put his arm around my shoulders and, intermittently shielding the sun from his eyes with his hand, pointed up at the mountain. And there it was, as clear as the daylight we were all unashamedly using up, the shape of a deer set deep in the mountain side, defined by the walls. It was the full size of this famous six-thousand-foot-high west side of Deer Mountain.

I smiled with relief, if not a little embarrassment, as finally something made sense. The man patted me on the back and returned to his family, leaving me staring up, wide-eyed at this phenomenon.

It was afternoon by the time I made it to the bottom of Deer Mountain, Monday afternoon I think! The sun was still out, shining in all its glory for the hikers. From the base of the mountain I could really appreciate the enormity of it, and it was truly quite breathtaking. It's difficult to imagine, I know, but the mountain side was actually quite flat; there was the gradual hill to the rear of the mountain that had provided my relatively easy journey to the top, which must be its east side, two nondescript north and south sides made up of fields, and then the west side with the deer tattoo which stood out as its focal point. The shape of the mountain was almost square at the base, and, although I couldn't even begin to guess its perimeter, it must have been several miles. The other thing you might be wondering is why the tattoo had been named as a deer. It is more acceptable to assume that the walls define some sort of recognisable shape that looks something like an animal, in the same way that the constellations do, but it usually takes a bit of direction and imagination to actually see what it is - join the dots so to speak. So how is it possible to create enough detail to leave no doubt whatsoever in anyone's mind that it is in fact a deer as opposed to any other animal? I don't know how I can answer that other than to say that you have to see it to believe it! And believe me, it was a deer! Its antlers broke up the enormous fields into smaller, randomly-shaped ones whilst appearing to support the entire mountain as though it were a small mound of dirt. Its body housed the large fields where the cattle grazed and its legs created four alternate pathways from the middle of the mountain to its base.

Although I was at the bottom of the mountain, and back on a regular, flat path, I was still overlooking some of the low valleys of the town. The paths continued to wind themselves downwards and the fields were now dotted with tiny stone cottages rather than animals.

There was also a neat row of four tents just to the left of the starting point of the path that led up Deer Mountain. I had noticed them during the final few steps of my descent, and hadn't as yet seen anyone go in or out of them. I thought it unlikely that people would be so keen to set off up the mountain so early in the morning that they had to camp at the bottom of it to get there quicker. After all, wouldn't the sun be accommodating enough to accompany a group of midnight hikers up the mountain, and how far away could they live? I could see most of the town from the top of the mountain, or so I thought. Anyway, I stood there for a while longer as I contemplated the next stage of my journey, which I hoped would take me down the valley and into the town centre.

It was the exceptionally loud sigh of relief that drew my attention back to the tents, and to what I soon learnt to be the shift changeover of the mountain lifeguard. Several other people gathered to watch as the current lifeguard shouted the next one on shift to get out of bed and prepared to pass over the life-saving equipment, which consisted of a fold-up seat, a large bottle of water, binoculars and a first-aid kit. The man just beginning his shift emerged from his tent in matching bright red combat trousers and a T-shirt that read 'Deer Mountain Guard' and began his climb up to the halfway point, which housed his viewing platform.

I was feeling quite exhausted by this time. I had already been walking for hours so, after watching the changing of the guard, I strolled along the path in no real hurry. I could see where I should be heading; the bottom of the valley gradually became the flat of the town centre and, although I could see it, it still seemed a very long walk away, so I took my time and then fell asleep, as I had done the previous night, before I reached my destination.

5

Iris Mennison

It was on my third day in Tunnelton, after a second night - I want to say sleeping rough but rough it certainly wasn't - sleeping in the warm climate of this beautiful countryside that now seemed as far from the Yorkshire Dales as the Australian outback, that I made it down to the valley, at the bottom of Deer Mountain, with the town centre in view.

The first building that caught my attention was a monorail station, and the first thing that struck me about it was that the platform itself was unusually at ground level; rather than having a lift to take passengers up to the track level, the track came down to the passengers' level. I stood and watched as a train pulled up alongside the solitary platform. The train was suspended from its track but also had wheels that set down onto the more familiar train track when it arrived at the platform. This track helped to bring the train down to ground level and guide it back up again. The train collected some passengers and then set off, climbing up to about fifty feet to join the suspended track that ran in figures of eight around the town. With the dips in the track down to the platforms, the slow climbs back up and the dodging of any tall buildings that got in its way, it looked more like a roller-coaster than a means of public transport. Surely I was not so surprised any more at Tunnelton's intricacies!

The roads here were quiet, and there were nowhere near as many people as I'd seen at Deer Mountain. I assumed that I wasn't far from the town centre because when the sun had gone down, or rather when the sun had been switched off, both during my walk up the hill and whilst I was lying down to sleep, this appeared to be where the mass of streetlights were, and of course there was the monorail, but apart from that it looked like any other town. Like I said before, there wasn't anything particularly strange about the place itself, or its inhabitants, it was more a feeling I got about it, and the fact that I just didn't know, in relation to anywhere else, where I was. Oh, and they did have some weird tourist attractions!

As I got closer to the monorail station, which I thought might be a good place to find a map, if such a thing existed, and maybe even a clue as to how to get home, I could see a few groups of schoolchildren forming on the platform. There were young kids and teenagers, chatting away and laughing. I wondered for a second whether to ask them about the town but all of a sudden I felt a bit silly for being lost there.

It was as the next train arrived that I noticed the children's clothes. Half of them were wearing a school uniform and the other half were wearing jeans, all exactly the same jeans. At first it didn't occur to me that ordinarily kids would be off school today, still on their Christmas break, but this turned out to be somewhat irrelevant. I quickly learnt that nothing ever closed or stopped running in Tunnelton, not even for Christmas.

What happened next was that the kids in school uniform got on the train, leaving the other kids in jeans waving from the platform. All sorts of explanations crossed my mind. Were the jeans another type of uniform for another school? Didn't these kids go to school? Were some of them from the town and some just visitors like me? I assumed at first that they must be waiting for another train, but shortly after they had waved goodbye they started walking off the platform towards the main road, towards me.

Before I go any further, let me describe the jeans to you, because they weren't just any kind of jeans. They were jet black, very baggy and flared at the bottom, covering their shoes and dragging behind on the ground. They had bright yellow double stitching and a logo on the back left-hand pocket in the same yellow thread.

It wasn't just a group of the younger kids or a group of the teenagers either, but a mixture of both, and now they all walked together, chatting away as if they were all brothers and sisters. As they got closer to me I dared myself to ask; as in the case of the mountain, these things are not always so obvious.

'Excuse me,' I called to one of the older kids as she walked past.

She seemed to be the leader of the group, probably about fourteen or fifteen, and rather embarrassingly slightly taller than me! She turned around.

'I just wanted to know about your jeans?' I asked. 'Is it some sort of uniform?'

The girl smiled and cleverly answered me with a question.

'You want to know why we're not at school today don't you?'

'Well yes, I suppose so,' I replied hesitantly. How funny it is that teenagers can be so self-confident, to the point of being quite intimidating.

'It's Iris Mennison Day,' she stated, 'but you probably don't know who she is do you?'

I shook my head and she continued.

'Iris Mennison is one of the greatest legends this town has ever seen. She was a singer, an actress, a teacher.' The girl's face lit up as she enjoyed telling me all about her idol.

'You see, religion, and by that I mean organised religion, is not so big here. Don't get me wrong; we all believe in God, I mean look around.' She lifted her hands to the sky. 'How could you not believe in God? But Iris Mennison, well, she's the one we worship, for bringing us happiness and entertainment, but most of all, imagination. Iris Mennison Day is the anniversary of her death, so if we're truly dedicated fans, and we can prove it by owning a pair of these jeans,' she said pointing down to her denim flares, 'then we get the day off school, like a bank holiday. If you keep your eyes open you'll probably see a few people off work today too. Just look for the yellow stitching.'

The girl laughed as she and her friends went skipping off towards the valley, the back pockets of their jeans all shining with *Iris* in yellow thread. I postponed my attempt to get home for another day.

6
Mindstream

'Where Drifting Minds Go' advertised the cartoon-like sign at the main gate of Tunnelton Park. It was a sunny afternoon as I took a stroll through the park, which I had come across during my search for the centre of the town. People were sunbathing or sat on benches reading or talking. Tennis matches and mini-golf were being played. Kids were splashing about in the shallow concrete swimming pool. I was still looking out for the jeans, and saw plenty hanging around the skate park and the ice-cream van. There was a toddlers' playground and a pony taking small children on a circuit of its field.

There didn't seem to be anything out of the ordinary, nothing that set it apart from any other park, and nothing that seemed to relate back to the sign at the gate.

I set off walking once again, hoping to discover on my travels some sort of explanation. I followed the main path that ran all the way around the park, decorated on each side with daffodils and tulips. I passed the eighteen-hole golf course on my left, then some more tennis courts on my right. It was a busy place with a lot of people out walking. Skateboards, roller-blades and BMX bikes went flying past me. The sun was out in full, and it looked nothing like the British winter up in that bright blue, cloudless sky.

The path eventually led me through a woodland area where the tall oak trees towered above me and the sun was blocked out completely for a couple of minutes by the dense forest that I had stumbled across.

When I made it out the other side, my eyes squinting at the sudden brightness of the sun, I brushed the leaves and the bark debris off my jacket and found myself standing in the middle of a field. At the end of the forest path there was a wooden sign nailed to the nearest tree; 'IN' it read, and over to the right was another wooden sign nailed to the neighbouring tree that read 'OUT'. Was this some sort of maze? Or someone's hiding place? I looked up at the oak trees again, this time from the edge of the forest, and could now see not just one but three or four immaculately crafted tree-houses. They were at varying heights; one of them was only about ten feet up the tree trunk with a ladder leading up to the door, but a couple of them appeared to be up in the clouds with no clue whatsoever of how to get up there.

The field I was in was a beautifully kept piece of land, with newly cut grass, colourful flowerbeds, wooden benches with gold-plated inscriptions on the back-rests, and a five-foot-square woodchipped area housing a solitary swing.

At first I couldn't see anyone around. There weren't any sunbathers there, or skateboarders, and there certainly weren't any kids. Well, there weren't any of the skater kids at least, just grown-up, sensible kids as I would soon find out. I was worried for a second that the sun would go in and leave me lost in this field because it just seemed so still, but then I remembered all the people I'd seen over on the other side of the park. Why was this side so hauntingly quiet? I couldn't decide whether to turn around, fight my way back through the forest and return quickly to the more populated area, or to set off, in this midst of greenery, in search of whatever it was I was looking for. You can probably guess; I went for the second option!

I like an adventure; you've probably guessed that too. If I were to say why I thought I'd ended up in Tunnelton, why I was chosen, if indeed that was the case, then I'd say it was for my sense of adventure. If I had arrived there by choice, say by winning a competition or completing the Tunnelton entrance exam, that's how I would have sold myself: adventurous nature, will travel!

I walked very quickly across the grass. I'm not sure whether I was scared, in a hurry, or just being impatient; it was probably all three. As I got halfway across the field, past the trees and bushes that had, up until now, been blocking my view over to the left, I could see at last where everyone was.

There was a theatre, out in the open; a small converted hut with a barn door at the back and a raised stage at the front. Within this modern-looking park, in a carefully nurtured field, stood this old makeshift theatre. It certainly had style and character, although it was in the process of falling apart. There was a hole in the roof and discarded planks of wood leant up against the side. It reminded me of something you might keep for sentimental reasons, knowing full well that you should just throw it out and buy a new one.

The audience occupied the four rows of seating in front of the stage. The chairs were a mixed collection of old wooden chairs, white plastic garden chairs, stripy deck-chairs and old school chairs with desks intact. Whatever it was they were watching, all forty or so of them were mesmerised by it. I spotted two empty seats, one in the very middle of the crowd, which I dismissed immediately, and one at the end of the back row. I crept over and sat down quietly, feeling rather lucky that my chair was an ordinary kind of wooden dining chair. I must admit that for the first few minutes of sitting there I was looking at who was in the audience rather than who was on the stage. It was an unusual mixture of people, quite a random selection of community, as if there was one person representing each age group and work sector. Then again, it's not as if I recognised anyone, so who was I to judge how the people of Tunnelton spent their free time?

Anyway, one act was just finishing, and as she exited via the flimsy steps at the front of the stage and disappeared round the back, I joined in with the applause and waited patiently for the show to continue.

The man sitting next to me looked typically French; by that I mean he looked almost too French to actually be French, like he was auditioning for a play and had overdone the research a little too much. He was sat on one of the old school chairs wearing blue jeans, patent black leather shoes, a white T-shirt and a brown suede jacket; oh, and a black beret! He was taking notes in a small ruled jotter, making use of the desk he was lodged into; that is, notes in French! Okay, first impressions proved to be right this time! I looked at him out of the corner of my eye so as not to invoke unwanted conversation. I decided to watch the show quietly for a while and hold back on the questions, thinking that maybe I would work it out for myself this time.

There was nothing on the stage, no backdrops or props, just a single microphone on a stand centre-stage. I took this to mean that it wasn't going to be a play as such, and as I hadn't heard any music so far I assumed it wasn't going to be a concert either.

After a silent two-minute pause, a boy walked round from behind the theatre, up the steps and stood confidently in front of the microphone as he lowered it to his height. He was a very smart, studious-looking young man, in a tailored suit and tie. He was about twelve years old, and a bit chubby with an unflattering bowl haircut. He was the exact opposite of the Iris Mennison skater kids. I wondered who he worshipped.

He looked a little bit sad for a minute, then he smiled and everyone in the audience smiled with him. He removed a small paperback book from the inside pocket of his jacket and with a shrug of his shoulders and a quick flick to brush aside the overgrown fringe from his eyes, announced,

'A modern interpretation of Descartes.'

It was incredible. In the ten minutes that he was stood up there he had the entire audience completely fixated on complex seventeenth-century philosophy. He finished with,

'Thank you for listening. My name is Joshua Simmons.'

The speakers marched onto the stage one by one, each holding on tightly to our attention for ten minutes.

Next was a woman of about sixty who began with,

'Marcus Aurelius - The man behind the emperor.'

A young man stood up to recite Plato's *Fables and Myths* off by heart. We had the honour of an eight-year-old girl simplifying Einstein's $E=mc^2$ on a hand-held chalkboard. Everything they said made perfect sense, and a thinker I may be, but an academic I'm certainly not.

After the last speaker had overcome his excitement about trigonometry versus calculus, the audience began to leave their seats and disperse into the park. The Frenchman beside me was just finishing off his notes, so I stood a little distance away from him, waited until he had closed his notepad and then began my questioning.

'Do you know any of these speakers we've seen here today?'

'Ahh,' he said shaking his head as he stood up straightening his jacket, 'it's a little bit complicated.'

He spoke to me very clearly in perfect English, but when he paused in between sentences I couldn't tell if he was waiting for me to say something or just contemplating his explanation. After he had adjusted his hat, stroked his beard and frowned a little he continued.

'You must think these people are, er...clever?'

'Well yes,' I nodded.

'That they are geniuses, yes?'

'I suppose so. I don't know any of that stuff.'

'They are, how do you say, disillusioned.'

I shook my head to indicate that I didn't really understand what he meant. He pointed to the chairs, suggesting we sit back down. This could take a while.

'You have seen the tree-houses?' he asked.

'Yes,' I replied.

'They are beautiful. Inside they are even better. Luxury with a view' he laughed.

'So that's where they live?' I asked during the next long pause, trying to push the conversation along. 'The speakers we just saw, they live up in the tree-houses do they?'

'Oh yes. They live up there with their books and their thoughts, enjoying conversation and the peacefulness of the park, away from the constrained brain-washing of television and music and their daily lives.'

'Their daily lives? I don't understand. Aren't their days spent here in the tree-houses like you just said?'

'Oh child,' he said to me as he patted my hand, although he wasn't much older than me. 'They're not really here, not in body, only in mind. Lost souls you may think, but lost they are not. In your world these are the people the system puts into psychiatric hospitals. It takes them away from their jobs, sometimes even their families, because it thinks they can't cope with the day-to-day running of the world. They don't understand wars and hatred, poverty and greed, ignorance or, well, stupidity, but let's face it, who does? They are clever, yes, but they have read too much, they understand too much, at least more than their peers, their medical do-gooders, the government maybe, even God perhaps. They are often found staring blankly at the television screen having frozen during the last bad news bulletin, lost in their own environment, or in many cases they just give in themselves, give up fighting the incomprehensible. They think they're crazy, they are led to believe that they are going mad when really it's just the world around them that's going mad.'

The man continued without any interruptions from me, and I was now hanging onto his every word.

'All those people you just saw on the stage are, at this moment in time, lying in bed, tucked up tightly with starched white sheets. Some of them are sedated, some remember their name, some don't, but they remember every word from every book they've ever read, and that's just about the only thing they understand, their knowledge. They always remember the facts and figures, just not the emotions.'

It would be fair to say I was pretty much in shock and more than a little scared at this point as I watched the speakers making their way back to the forest, the maze, forming an orderly queue at the 'IN' gate.

'It's like Heaven,' I said, speaking my thoughts out loud.

'Not Heaven,' the man began again. 'Your idea of Heaven is that people die, their bodies are buried and their souls live on in Heaven. Is that correct?'

'I guess so.'

'These people are far from being dead, and this place, this town, as difficult as it is to get to, does actually exist. Now don't get me wrong, I believe in God and Heaven and all that stuff, but death, well in particular the after-life, is still very much just an idea isn't it? A belief. It's not somewhere you can visit and return from is it? You see, the speakers we just saw, their bodies are in your world, alive and healthy, it's just that their minds have drifted into this world for a little while. But don't worry, most of the time body and mind are reunited.'

The man stood up again and I did the same.

'Now it's been a pleasure talking to you, er...'

'Paddy.'

'Paddy, and I'm René. But if you don't mind I have to be on my way.'

'Well thank you for your time.'

'You're very welcome.'

'Do you live here then?' I couldn't resist asking him. I wanted to know how he knew all this stuff. Was it because he himself was a wandering soul?

'I'm just on my way back,' he replied, and, tapping his notepad with his pen, said. 'I've just figured it out. You have to do when you've got kids.'

He waved goodbye, first of all to me and then to the last of the speakers heading for the trees, and when I turned back to him he was just disappearing out of sight round the back of the theatre.

7
Lost Property

As you can imagine, I left Tunnelton Park rather quickly following my meeting with René. I was determined now to find the most populated area of the town and get some real answers about what I was doing there. I had spent my first night indoors since arriving in Tunnelton, in a basic motel on the edge of the park. I'm saying motel rather than hotel because that's exactly what it was, the difference I believe being that in a motel the rooms are accessed from the outside and in a hotel from the inside. What had happened was that I had found myself in an area just outside the park that I now like to refer to as *Little America*. It wasn't like the 1950s America I had encountered in Mrs Featherstone's kitchen, this was present-day American style, and this time it wasn't just one building but the entire street.

Anyway, I checked in to the motel, although it was free, with a recommended contribution to 'Our Schools and Wildlife' with which I happily complied. The idea was that you either signed up to help out in the gardens, doing which ever odd jobs needed doing or you wrote a few words that were then added to an on-going book that was passed around the schools and hospitals. I enjoyed writing a paragraph or two about my first impressions of Tunnelton and how it compared to my home town. I then had a good night's sleep in room 42 of Parkside. That's all it said on the neon sign, 'Parkside'. Maybe the bulbs had gone out on the word 'Motel'; they usually have in films, haven't they?! Horror films that is! Anyway it was there that I managed to get my clothes washed. They were collected from my room and returned washed, ironed and folded in the morning. I also acquired, as an additional welcome gift from the hotel owner, a rather unflattering T-shirt to wear in the meantime which boasted a memorable photograph of the motel. I felt every bit the tourist that I was!

So I was out of the park, and I was in the town centre, what next? The streets were getting busy as I was enjoying a morning stroll along the main road the following day. I stopped off for breakfast in a diner called Breakfast Square. Everything was so exhaustingly American all the way along the street; the motel, the pedestrian crossings with signs saying 'No Jaywalking' then giving you four seconds exactly to cross over six lanes of revving engines at the sight of the green 'Walk' sign. The bottomless cup of coffee and the all-you-can-eat breakfast buffet, however, I liked! I ate as many sausages, hash browns and slices of toast as I could fit in. After all, I had a long day ahead of me, no doubt filled with all kinds of surprises!

I couldn't quite get my head around the money situation. I knew about the solar power, and therefore no electricity bills. I knew about the donations to charity in lieu of payment in places such as hotels and restaurants, sorry, motels and diners around here! But surely everyone out working got paid? The public transport, the schools and shops seemed to run as normal. It couldn't be such a perfect place that people worked for free could it? Everything was free but everyone worked for free, would that work? I asked the waiter when he next came over to fill up my coffee.

'How do I pay for this?' I asked him, at which he swung around and handed me a visitor's book.

'Just sign this' he said, 'and make some kind of comment about the food or service. Or just tell a joke!'

'Okay' I nodded. 'Do you mind if I ask though, how do you all get paid if you don't use money? Does everyone really work for free?' I asked, hoping it wasn't an inappropriate question.

'Yes' he replied, 'as long as everyone is willing to do their share of work, and no-one is greedy when it comes to material goods, then yes it works.'

What an unusual, but refreshing concept I thought to myself as the waiter moved on to the next table. It certainly wouldn't work in our world.'

After breakfast I continued my walk along the main road, which took me round a bend, out of sight of the park and suddenly everything became very British again. Dual carriageways met up from opposing directions and wound their way into a nightmare of a one-way system. I thought this was going to be it; this would be where I would finally see someone here lose their patience, get into a bit of road rage with the sound of car horns and swearing, but no. The inhabitants of Tunnelton had, as yet, not shown me human traits such as impatience, anger and vanity. They were very calm, and as a result of that, so was I.

Now I know I keep saying that the town looked pretty much like any other town - there were roads, cars, hotels, restaurants, and ordinary people - but the town centre wasn't at all like any other town centre I'd ever seen. The main difference, if you can imagine this, was that there weren't any familiar shops. You know what I mean, it wasn't your average kind of modern high street with instantly recognisable chain store names. Judging it first of all by the buildings, there were single-storey stone buildings, wooden-fronted townhouses and redbrick skyscrapers. It was yet again a combination of decades, of eras, this time of periods of architecture, and this was my speciality. I'd never seen such an array of examples on display in one place, and I could describe them all - my university lecturers would have been proud!

The town didn't have a particular theme to it or a particular feel, but, although the shops that were there were more like local, family-run shops rather than big-name high-street stores, it didn't exactly feel old-fashioned either. There was a large pebbled square on which stood a twice-the-life-size monument of Iris Mennison. I took a closer look at it. In this sculpture she was a woman of about sixty with thick wavy hair and an infectious grin on her face. She was posing with one leg in front of her and the other leg bent backwards as if she might be running for the bus. I thought that the steel placard screwed to the base of the statue might tell me some more but it was simply inscribed in large yellow letters with 'Iris Mennison' and then underneath in small, neatly carved capital letters 'DREAMER'.

The shops may not have been big money-making stores but there was certainly no shortage of them. The tens of shops selling groceries, fresh bread and pastries, knitwear, hand made board games, along with the cobblers, the tailors and the cafés, stood there neatly in parallel lines with several pebbled streets running away at a tangent. I was also finally amongst the mass of streetlights that I had seen from various viewing points previously on my journey, and there were a lot of them. At about twenty-five feet tall, the black, ornamental lamp posts towered above the ground with each alternate one displaying a hanging basket on a hook about halfway down. Of course the lights weren't on; there were hundreds of people walking around the town, keeping the sun busy.

I suppose it's sounding like an old-fashioned town isn't it? Going to a grocery store for your weekly supply of personally weighed out fresh vegetables and treat of canned goods that are handed to you from a dusty shelf behind the counter, then having to go next door for your bread, and somewhere else entirely for milk. Well, it either sounds old-fashioned or very similar to Hepby! The people, although they all looked relatively normal, only stood out slightly because of their rather old-fashioned clothes, or at the very least, as my trendy young cousins would say, they were 'a little last season'! So imagine you're walking along the dainty cobbled streets. Now imagine it with cars, traffic lights, people on mobile phones. Confusing? Believe me it is!

So like I said, there were plenty of people about, shopping or meeting for coffee. It was all rather pleasant, cars but no road rage, shoppers but no pushing, no lunchtime rush, no queuing. What was the matter with this place? It's funny how a calm environment slows you down, takes away the panic and the twenty-first century instinct of needing to do everything now. There was certainly no sense of urgency to be detected there, no rush culture.

Every day so far I had set out with the intention of finding out the answers to my three questions: Where am I? What am I doing here? How do I get home? Yet there was something about the atmosphere of the place that, once I was out there breathing the Tunnelton air, made it seem not so important any more. My pangs of guilt, as I knew I should be at work, were quickly dampened by the calmness of the place, and, most importantly of all, I was having a lovely time there. Surely life's too short for worrying?

As usual I just kept on walking. I took notice of the shops, admired their window displays and artistic hand-painted signs hanging above the doors. In fact when I stepped back to take in the full atmosphere of Tunnelton town centre, it reminded me very much of a film set; how the scenery for a costume drama, for example, might be slotted in between the busy roads of a cosmopolitan city. The wooden signs tacked up over the new plastic printed ones, designer clothes having been removed from shop windows to be replaced by a 'Tailors - by appointment only'. But it wasn't a film set. This was Tunnelton, my new home for the time being, and I liked it just the way it was.

At the end of the high street the road split into two. The road to the left led you past a few more shops and eventually to another monorail station, whilst the road to the right, which of course I took because it looked more interesting, led me down to a single, very large building which stood alone, without a path leading up to it, without a pavement beside it or a garden around it. It was just there at the end of the shop-free street where the town centre, if not the entire town itself, appeared to end. The three-storey stone building, wide enough for the six double windows of each floor to occupy the front wall, stood contentedly across the width of the street, creating a dead-end.

It had the aura of a stately home, the regal touch of a castle, although at a guess it would now most probably be a public service building of some kind: government headquarters turned into a police station, a late countesses home now an elite boarding school, or, the worst possible scenario, a fallen bank converted into a café bar! It wasn't any of these obviously; that would just be too simple wouldn't it? It was, however, the most interesting place I had been to so far.

I walked straight in, as the heavy-duty door was already open. I followed the corridor all the way down to the back of the building, leaving aside for now my curiosity about the three closed red doors to my left and the spiral stone staircase to my right. The corridor led me to a large reception room where a rather overweight, middle-aged man in an exceptionally smart three-piece suit, complete with pocket watch and silk handkerchief, stood behind a solid oak, waist-high desk extending the width of the room. Bearing in mind that the width of the room was two walls short of the width of the building, that's a lot of desk! Behind him was a single shelf suspended from the concrete wall by metal chains. On it were twenty-six grey lever arch files. I didn't count them, I could just see that there was one for each letter of the alphabet, and they were supported by two wooden bookends, one in the shape of the letter A, its partner in the shape of the letter Z. How organised! But what was in them? There was also a large sign hung on the wall that read, 'Lost Property', and it sparkled silver and gold under the fluorescent lighting. In the centre of the desk, in front of the man who now had his back to me studying something beginning with R, was a gold-plated bell with the word 'Enquiries' engraved on the side.

The man turned around and with a low, cheery voice greeted me with,

'Yes sir, how may I help you?' He leaned over the desk, both palms pressed firmly down on the surface as he looked at me over his reading glasses.

'I've actually just come for a look around,' I answered genuinely. This could do no harm I thought, he can only say no. 'I noticed this building from the high street and I had to find out what it was.'

'Anything in particular you would like to see sir?' the man continued politely.

'Not really,' I replied.

At this he pressed the bell on the desk with a bouncy, comical action. This brought to the desk a similar-looking man, yet a much slimmer and younger version, in an identical suit. I thought he might be one of the guides, sent to show me around. Either that or he was a well-dressed security guard sent to show me out.

'Rupert,' the older man bellowed, rolling the R, 'would you mind the desk for me please. I am going to take this young gentleman on a little tour.'

'Certainly Mr Adams,' Rupert replied, and I could have sworn out of the corner of my eye I saw him bow.

'Now then,' Mr Adams said, turning his attention back to me as he walked to the end of the long desk and squeezed himself out through the insufficient gap at the end, 'where shall we start?'

I shook my head.

'Always best to start at the top and work your way down.'

'I thought the saying went, always best to start at the bottom and work your way up?' I answered back, a little hesitantly.

Mr Adams laughed. It could almost have been a hysterical laugh had it not been for the fits of coughing that calmed him down. He pressed the button for the lift on the wall to my right, and then he laughed some more.

'What's your name son?' he asked.

'It's Paddy, Paddy Jones.' I almost added 'sir' but I caught myself. He just had that teacher-like authority about him, but he looked like a hotel manager and he had the craziest laugh. His young protégé, Rupert, shuffled papers behind the desk frantically like a newly hired office junior in his dad's suit. Mr Adams removed his glasses and cleaned them with his handkerchief, still chuckling to himself.

'Paddy,' he said patting my shoulder as the lift beeped on arrival, 'I like you Paddy.'

The lift took us up to the third floor, the top floor. I followed Mr Adams along the corridor to the left, as he hummed to himself and jangled the keys in his pocket. We passed several doors on either side of the corridor; they were all painted a glossy red that perfectly matched the red carpet under our feet. It looked like a hotel corridor, the only exception being that none of the doors were labelled; there weren't any room numbers or signs on the doors at all.

We finally arrived at the desired, anonymous red door and Mr Adams swiftly found the key on his over populated keyring to let us in. I soon realised once we were inside the room that all the doors we had just passed, in fact all the doors on this floor, must just open out into this vast space. I didn't ask Mr Adams why he had chosen that particular red door as our entrance to the room, I just marvelled at the sheer size of it, one room that filled the entire top floor.

The length of the corridor, which housed the lift, the stairs and the endless entrance doors, created the ceiling support in the centre of the room. The rest of the floor was open-plan, minimalist even. The four outer walls were covered completely with bookcases, boarding up any windows that were there, and leaving the dazzling fluorescent strip-lighting to create a whiter than white artificial mist. The bookcases were light oak, the same as the floorboards, and they ran from ceiling to floor for the entire circuit of the room. It was only the corridor-length pillar in the centre of the room that prevented you from spinning round and seeing it all at once, which was probably a good thing - the size of the room alone made me a little dizzy.

Every compartment on the wall was labelled and stacked neatly. The letters A to H were printed in black on large, square white boards suspended with chains from the ceiling. These were the column headings that directed you around the room. Underneath each one the shelves listed the type of item that was stored there. I couldn't possibly tell you about them all, as I didn't have nearly enough time to look all the way around.

A few of the shelves caught my eye though, and it was as if Mr Adams could predict which ones they would be because he pointed them out to me before I got the chance to ask.

'Christmas cards,' he said pointing to a shelf of brightly coloured envelopes, 'lost in the post.'

'Footballs kicked over into next-doors garden.' We were walking back towards the entrance door.

'Hats.' He concluded with, 'Always an increase in lost hats in wintertime,' as he opened that same red door for me. At least I think it was the same door.

We went down to the second floor in the lift only to find that it was an exact replica of the top floor, well apart from the column headings, which this time read from I to P. Every item of property anyone could possibly lose was carefully filed in its rightful place in this building.

'Jewellery,' Mr Adams pointed out. 'Keys,' he continued, 'so, so many keys', as he shook his head.

'Laptop computers left on buses, oh yes,' he nodded. 'Mobile phones, switched off thank goodness.'

Then we came to the post, not just a shelf but a whole column all to itself.

'Christmas cards are separated,' Mr Adams explained. 'We're a bit sentimental like that. This here is just your regular lost post, lots of cheques funnily enough.'

Just as we were about to depart the second floor, I noticed a sign to the left of the door that said 'Pets - Outside', with an arrow pointing towards the only window in the room that was not boarded up, and then it was only a space in the bookcase that had been cut out to make it see-through.

'Pets?' I exclaimed.

'This way,' Mr Adams replied, showing me to the tiny

window that was within one of the pigeonholes created by the shelving on the back wall. Outside, a garden extension had been built. It was at second-floor level, a patio raised up off the ground by four concrete posts, with areas of grass, trees and woodchip, and the garden itself fenced in for safety. I was looking for animals but all I could see were rows of water bowls and a sort of self-service food machine that worked on the instructions of a paw.

'Mostly cats,' Mr Adams explained, peering over my shoulder. 'The odd delinquent dog or adventurous hamster,' he laughed, 'but mostly cats.'

Down on the first floor we entered the Q to Z database from one of the doors I had passed on my way in. This room was obviously not quite as big as the others as it had to accommodate the reception desk area, but it still contained an impressive selection of suitcases, train tickets and wallets.

When we returned to the front desk, Rupert was leaning against it with his back to us enjoying a cup of tea that he had discreetly made for himself in our absence.

'Rupert,' Mr Adams' loud, cheery voice resounded. Rupert jumped and turned around immediately, spilling some of his tea in the process. 'That will be all thank you Rupert.'

Rupert and Mr Adams swapped places and Mr Adams reached under the desk for what can only be described as a souvenir brochure. It was in full colour with a detailed map of the building and an alphabetical list of lost property items.

'How long do you keep all these things for then?' I asked him.

'Well, you'd be surprised how many items are returned to their rightful owners every year, especially expensive jewellery, things like that, and the inexpensive items we keep for about a year unless we get particularly attached to them, like the cats, and then they just stay.'

'So how do the owners reclaim their property? Do they have to come here? Is this just Tunnelton's lost property?'

'Oh no', Mr Adams exclaimed, setting off on another laughing and coughing fit, 'we're not that forgetful here! No, these belongings come from every corner of the Earth. They're sent to us by the kind people who bother to pick up a pair of gloves dropped in the street, and the honest bar staff who don't keep mobile phones left in the toilets for themselves. All people have to do to claim them is fill in a form at the post office with the details of the item they have lost and their address and we kindly return it to them. Simple.' He clapped his hands together as if he had just finished an important speech and stared at me with an 'Any questions?' look. I just smiled back, thanked him for the tour and the brochure and, of course, another contribution to my increasing knowledge of Tunnelton.

8
The Open Book

It was lunchtime by the time I left Lost Property HQ, and I
was starving. I got fish and chips in return for a drawing of
my parents' house back in Hepby, and ate them on the way
to the monorail station. Now, this form of transport was new
to me, as was the concept of not having to buy a ticket, but
you shouldn't complain about a free holiday with unlimited
travel should you?! I waited on the platform, finishing off my
chips and as I wasn't heading anywhere in particular I
jumped on the first train that arrived. The trains comprised
just two carriages each, but inside they reminded me very
much of the London Underground trains. They had rows of
seats set against both sides and plenty of bars and handles to
hold on to. I knew this was going to be a rocky journey so I
sat down and held on tightly. The train began its climb up to
cruising height and then gave me quite a pleasant overview
of my journey so far. I saw the high street and the park from
an aerial view, then the fields and the mountains. I stayed on
the train past all the areas I recognised and when it finally
came to a stop in a small but busy village area I chose to get
off the train and have a look around.

I suppose it isn't really an accurate description to call it a
village, but then the town centre was little more than a single
high street itself. This area was village-like in that there were
a few little streets grouped together comprising terraced
houses, shops and a café. It also had a school, a library, a
church and its fair share of fields and sheep. I thought that
if I didn't find anything to do there then it wasn't too late to

head back to the town centre or the American motel. The train journey had only taken five minutes. Basically, everywhere in the town was within easy walking distance.

I had a nice walk around the village streets, taking in another good dose of the countryside, and then I sat down in the café and collected my thoughts of the day over a cappuccino.

The town was almost starting to feel like home. The thought of going back to normality, back to my dingy flat and, in comparison to my recent adventures, relatively boring job, appealed to me less and less each day. Then I realised that I hadn't thought about the date since I'd arrived and, after having to calculate it very slowly, I worked out that it must be New Year's Eve. I hadn't really been thinking about what day it was, and seeing as my watch still wasn't working I had become less interested in the time as well. Thinking back to the Daylight-Saving explanation, I wondered whether there would be some other kind of crazy rule for the date too. Maybe Tunnelton ran according to its own calendar; it certainly ran according to its own rules! As far as I was concerned it was just another day of my journey, a journey of who knows how long. I figured I wasn't very likely to be invited to any New Year's Eve celebrations, so the date didn't mean anything to me either. I would just do my own thing and find something else to occupy my curious mind.

The village library was my next stop. The front of the library was only the width of one of the terraced houses, but the entrance was a heavy, wooden double-door, one side of which was propped open with a fire extinguisher. I walked in and saw that there were a few other people milling around, some sat reading, some sat writing and some were picking up and putting down every book on the shelves twice.

I had a wander round and then selected a few books at random from the shelves. I didn't recognise any of the titles so it really was a lucky dip.

At the back of the library there were five desks facing the wall with a division between each one so that you couldn't see the person you were sitting next to. There was a young woman sitting in the booth on the left and a man sat at the desk in the middle, so naturally I went to the booth on the right, leaving a spare desk between each of us. There wouldn't be any cheating in this exam!

I opened up the first book called *White Ground* by N. S. Field. I read the first couple of pages, then had a quick flick through the rest. As my eyes briefly scanned the pages of this short book I had to go back and double check that, yes, it really did finish in the middle of chapter three, and in the middle of a sentence too, leaving the rest of the pages completely blank. It was strange because it was bound together with a hardback cover but yet was unfinished. I skimmed through the other three books I had picked up only to find that they followed exactly the same pattern. I had a *Third Book of Poems* by Cecil Abbott, which contained just two completed verses and stopped before the end of the third, a children's book that contained pencil sketches and a large capital letter in a box ready to begin each chapter but no words adjoining it, and, last but not least, a Mediterranean recipe book that presented a list of ingredients needed for each dish but never went on to explain how to cook them.

I got up from the desk to have a quick look at a few other books to see if they were all the same before I projected my questions at the librarian, and found that they were all incomplete.

The librarian, a woman in her early sixties, with a permed bob, a pleated skirt and a Christmas jumper, had already noticed the confused look on my face and said hello to me as I approached the counter.

'Are all the books in here unfinished then?' I jumped in with really my only question.

The woman nodded, as if really that was obvious.

'Why?' I tried again for an explanation.

'Unfinished doesn't necessarily mean they're not worth reading. People die in the middle of their most beautiful poem or their most powerful novel. It's inspiring, particularly the ones that have just been found abandoned in a house move, or thrown away even, without a name to relate them to or an address to send them back to.'

'Oh okay,' I smiled, happy with that information for now. As I turned to leave the library, the woman surprised me slightly by adding in a much louder voice than before. 'The ending isn't always important. It's the fact that there is a beginning that counts.'

I wondered if she was talking about my journey through Tunnelton. She looked like the kind of person who knew more than her words revealed.

9
South of Heaven

I must admit to being a little surprised to discover a church in the village because it was the first church I'd seen since I'd arrived, and there it was, tucked out of the way in such a tiny village. I remembered the story of Iris Mennison and had got the impression that in this town faith was more of a personal thing than a shared community event, but even that turned out to be not entirely true.

The church was a small, dark chapel, and it looked very, very old, even for a church. I couldn't see any lights shining through the windows, and there weren't any bells ringing or any people waiting outside the closed door, but as I got closer and stopped to listen more carefully I was sure I could hear a choir.

Should I creep inside? I thought, sit at the back quietly and just wait for something to happen? No. I decided against that idea. Curiosity was one thing, but I didn't want to start breaking any rules or disrespecting a religious place or its people.

A little bit tired of walking, I sat down on the front step of the church, pulled my jacket around me and rubbed my hands together; it was getting a bit chilly. I hadn't seen anyone else around for quite some time, and after I'd been sat down for five minutes or so, the sun went in.

I must have been sat there for a while with my head in my hands. I wasn't feeling unhappy, but as it was New Year's Eve it was the first time I'd felt a bit homesick, thinking that I'd usually be out with my friends by now or enjoying a village street party back in Hepby. Anyway, when I lifted up my head, rubbing my eyes and stretching my arms I noticed first of all that the sun was out again and the church bells were ringing, but secondly that there was a group of people standing in front of me waiting for the doors to open. None of them asked me who I was or what I was doing there, but when I stood up to move to the back of the crowd out of the way, one or two of them gave a friendly hello.

The doors were opened about ten minutes later by a man in a long white gown. I assumed that this was going to be a church service like any other, a chance for the community to gather, say their prayers, sing some hymns and, as I believed that it must be New Year's Eve, I thought there were worse places I could be so I followed the crowd inside.

I was handed a service booklet on my way through the inner door by one of the choirboys assigned with his duties for the evening. I was then ushered to a seat in the second row. The church was filling up rapidly, mostly with mothers and young children, but with a few elderly people and dads thrown into the balance, a very similar audience make-up to the one Hepby church saw at the Christmas Eve carol concert. The room was filling up from the back, just like a classroom. I worried that they knew something I didn't. Maybe the vicar singled out people in the first two rows to answer questions or help with the breaking of the bread.

As it was such a small church, the six rows of pews, divided down the middle by a narrow, red-carpeted aisle, were set close together leaving you very little leg room. There was a raised section for the choir but even this provided standing room only behind the two book ledges that stood facing each other. The rest of the fixtures and fittings looked rather familiar. There was a large table set with a white tablecloth and silver candleholders at the head of the aisle but below the raised section that created the altar. There was a wooden board hanging on the left-hand wall at the front with what I supposed were hymn numbers slotted into it, a pulpit for the readings and the visible pipes of a church organ, albeit a very small one, the organist tucked away out of sight.

I sat there patiently and skimmed through the four-page service booklet. On the cover it simply said 'Welcome to Tunnelton Church Wednesday Evensong'. This told me two things. First of all, this sub-village obviously didn't have a name of its own; the town in its entirety must be just Tunnelton, and secondly, it must be New Year's Eve because the booklet had confirmed the day as Wednesday, even though it hadn't given the date. Maybe they just didn't celebrate it? This knowledge reassured me a little, because perhaps, after all, this was just a small town with its one church, hidden away somewhere but not a million miles from civilisation as I knew it.

Shortly after everyone had taken their seats and the children had settled down, the church bells stopped chiming and the church organist began playing a rather personalised rendition of the introduction to Stravinsky's *Le Sacre du Printemps*. I recognised this because we had studied it at school, but what an unusual choice for a church service! To this the fourteen choirboys marched in twos to their positions on the stage. The organist then gave a short pause before pounding rather clumsily into the first hymn. It was a hymn I recognised but I couldn't tell you what it was called. I found the words to it inside the cover of the booklet I had been given and I stood up to sing when everyone else did as the vicar made his slow pilgrimage to the altar. I don't really know how to describe him. He looked like a vicar, standing in his robes behind the altar, an elderly man with wispy white hair that, although probably not intentionally, made him look slightly eccentric, although to describe him as a vicar somehow doesn't fit in with the rest of the service, but we'll leave him as the vicar for now.

So, yes, this was an ordinary looking church, with a man who appeared to be a vicar, a choir and hymns, but the similarity to Hepby church ended there.

As we all sat down after the first hymn, leaving the vicar and the choir standing, a woman from the front row passed her child to its father and, with a nod from the vicar, climbed up the steps to the pulpit. It wasn't like our church where you need a microphone so the people at the back and up on the balcony can hear you; the woman just raised her voice a little and the words echoed around the building. She smiled back at her happy audience and began her personally penned reading.

'I'm sure everyone will agree that we are very lucky to live in this beautiful place.' There were a few nods and a lot more smiling.

'We have been given the privilege of living in an unspoilt landscape, the safety of a community that has no reason for war. We are protected from the things we don't understand, the *bad things*, as we say to our children!' A few laughs from the mums.

'Maybe it would be better if we didn't know what went on outside our happy world, but if we didn't, if we turned off the news to protect ourselves and our children from pain and suffering, we would surely not be able to do many of the things that our community does to help. I ask you today to pray for those less fortunate than ourselves and to find the strength within yourselves to open your eyes to the bigger picture and do whatever you can to help.' With this, the woman smiled, stepped down and returned to her family to an appreciative applause.

Then we began the second hymn, *All Things Bright and Beautiful*. I knew this one! After which it was the vicar's turn to speak, and for this we remained standing.

'Let me begin by thanking each and every one of you for joining me here today. It is such a pleasure to see the community come together like this, to say our thanks, to pray, to teach our children, and if I may also say, our visitors.' I'm sure he looked at me, and just for a second we caught each other's eye, as I assumed he recognised everyone there except me. He paused to regain his train of thought, 'And to teach our children all about this truly wondrous place we call home.' He took off his glasses and had a sip of water. 'Please sit,' he whispered.

For a couple of minutes he rested his body, leaning over the altar, and rested his voice as we all waited patiently in silence. When he stood up straight again, he lifted up his arms as if embracing the audience and raised his voice.

'Tunnelton is not a figment of our imagination. It is not removed completely from the confines of the Earth. It is hidden, yes, but it is not inaccessible, it is not a secret. It has answers but your questions should always be relevant, respectful and to the point.' Again I'm sure he looked at me, with my twenty questions for anyone who'd listen. Why couldn't I have found a seat on the back row?!

'All I ask of you,' he said, concluding his speech, 'is that you do whatever it takes to make yourself happy. Free your imagination. Reach for your goals. Stand in the face of adversity and negativity and knock them down with your strength of mind. Most of all,' he paused to take another sip of water and clear his throat, 'never ever give up on your dreams.'

The congregation clapped again. Applause isn't something I've come to expect in a church but I must say that it makes it a much more pleasant experience. After the choir and the vicar had reversed their journey back down the aisle, I mingled in with the crowd, trying to remain inconspicuous. I could see the vicar standing outside, shaking hands with his followers. I wondered whether he would stop me and ask me what I was doing there, so I slowed down a bit, trying to wait until he was deep in conversation with someone else so I could slip past him unnoticed. I took one last look around the entrance hall. There were a few coats hanging up and a noticeboard giving details of local events. Then I noticed, on the back of the door, an inscription, not on a placard but actually carved into the wood, a quote from the woman herself. It read,

I've been found somewhere North of Hell
To the left of innocence
On my right an angel with the devil
I'm somewhere South of Heaven.

Underneath was a print of her signature, 'Iris Mennison - Still Dreaming!'

When I eventually left the entrance hall the vicar did stop me and he shook my hand, but he didn't ask me any questions. He just pointed back up to the door and said, 'The idea of Heaven and Hell is not so easily explained when you live in a place like this. Many visitors think this is Heaven; the thinkers over in the park believe it's even higher than Heaven. We like to believe that when a dreamer dies, like Iris Mennison, their dreams don't die with them. They have enough power of their own to float around in our galaxy, still learning, still finding their way around. If the body is buried, does the soul have to go to either Heaven or Hell? And who decides? Or can it still be free, in a vacuum between the two? Iris Mennison didn't want to go to Heaven, she always wanted the top, the highest point, wherever that may be, to be always slightly out of reach, then she would always have something to do, something to aspire to. The poem you just read she wrote just before she died, so that's where we believe she is, just south of Heaven. Almost but not quite. The waiting teaches you more than the arrival.' He shook my hand again. 'Thank you for coming to the service today.'

'It was my pleasure,' I replied as I set off towards the gate.

'Oh and Happy New Year,' he shouted after me.

I turned around and smiled. It was the first time I'd heard anyone say that in Tunnelton.

'Happy New Year,' I shouted back to him.

10
Tug of War

After leaving the church I found a little hostel round the back of the café I had visited earlier. It was nothing special, just a set of bunk beds in a bare room with a communal bathroom, but as I was the only guest that night I had quite a comfortable stay and even a hot shower.

In the morning I walked round to the café for a cup of coffee and a doughnut. I was served by the same woman as the day before, which provided a welcome feeling of familiarity. As it was quiet in the café, the woman brought over a cup of coffee for herself and joined me at the round plastic table with its blue and white checked tablecloth and matching seat cushions. She introduced herself as Lorrie. We chatted for ten minutes or so about very ordinary, mundane things like the weather, the coffee, and the interior design of the café. I never thought to ask why it was open on New Year's Day, but it looked like everywhere was running as normal; no bank holidays here, maybe because there weren't any banks! Then she started asking me where I'd visited since I'd been in Tunnelton. Had I been to the church? Yes. Had I been to the library? Yes. The park? The American Quarter? The town centre? Yes. Yes. Yes. Then she asked me if I'd been to the war museum.

'War museum?' I exclaimed. 'Surely there's never been a war here?' My mind boggled. What reason could there have ever been for a war? And between who? The woman in the church had even spoken about it being a place with no reason for war.

'No of course there has never been a war here,' Lorrie reassured me.

Lorrie was like a grown-up cheerleader. She was probably about fifty but she wore her peroxide blonde hair in pig tails with permanently set make-up and a white waitress's apron over her short skirt, glittery top and knee-high black boots. She did look a little bit over-dressed for a village café with its one customer, but she was friendly, she was extraordinarily happy and she kept bringing me more coffee and doughnuts so I liked her! She returned to the counter every so often to make a coffee to take out or put a sandwich and a piece of flapjack in a paper bag but despite the distractions we were sat talking for a good hour. She went on to tell me about the war museum, and it was at this point that, regardless of her chosen uniform, she sounded much too intelligent to be wasting her time making coffee.

'It's not a museum of war exactly, although it holds a lot of historical information about it. The way to look at it,' she explained, sipping her coffee, 'is like a seesaw. It explains the reasoning behind war, the options that were available at the time and why the decision to go to war on each occasion was made. Then it shows you all the positive, inspiring and truly great things that happened parallel to each war. It balances it out, the good and the bad.'

'So it's easier to understand why the really terrible things happen?'

'Yes, and not just war. War is just a good example. For instance, when there's war in one country there might be blissful peace in another. War can often create peace. You might think that's obvious, that's the idea, right? But you have to look at the bigger picture. Try to think that for every death there's a birth, for every tear there's a smile. Small things maybe, but it's no less important that they are balanced out.'

'What about murder?' I asked.

Lorrie admired her nails whilst she thought about the answer.

'I'm afraid we haven't found a counterweight for that one yet kid.' And with that she returned to the counter to serve a hot chocolate, looking a little drained of the optimism she had passed on to me. The war museum would be my next stop.

The war museum was situated halfway between the village and the town centre. Lorrie had told me to look out for a little stream that ran below the monorail track near to the Tunnelton Park stop. I found it peacefully trickling away by yet another entrance gate to the park. I crossed over on the rope bridge as instructed, although it wasn't exactly a long way across, or the water very deep for that matter, but I did it the correct way. It would seem that entering the museum's grounds by balancing on a rope bridge was all part of the war museum experience, plus if you've got muddy shoes from taking a shortcut through the stream, they won't let you in.

The building itself stood in its own private area of Tunnelton Park. I had certainly not noticed it the last time I had been in the park. It wasn't a particularly large building; in fact it was really just a bungalow, all built at ground level. The flowers grew in neat, straight lines that created a path from the end of the bridge over the stream to the front door. Maple trees stood at either side of the doorway and ivy crept up the walls and embraced the windows.

'Six of One, Half a Dozen of the Other' stated the wooden sign that was only just keeping its balance alongside a couple of pot plants on the outer windowsill.

This sign was one of many that caught my attention on this

visit, and they were all painfully well-meaning and thought-provoking; forgotten sayings, old wives' tales and predictable clichés I suppose, but somewhat heart-warming and fitting for my visit, not only to the museum but for my entire visit to Tunnelton.

I didn't pay to enter the museum but I got a ticket to add to my collection of souvenirs. I didn't get a personal tour guide there either, I was just told to follow the green arrows on the floor. It was nice in a way to wander round at my own pace, taking in all the displays, reading the memoirs and passing by the repetitive photographs of tanks and aeroplanes. It was all very interesting but some of it was very bleak and harrowing. It was the first display of pain and suffering that I'd seen in Tunnelton and, although I knew the reasoning behind it, I did have to restrain myself a little from rushing on to the happy stuff.

There were literally thousands of passport-sized photographs of soldiers who had died in World War One, creating a mosaic effect on one huge wall in the main hall, the wall opposite displaying the soldiers lost in World War Two. There were books that were full of messages of thanks, condolences and memories, all of which had been carefully laminated to preserve them through time.

There were framed newspaper cuttings, headlines from every natural and man-made disaster the world had ever seen. There were medals and uniforms in glass cases, and news flashes and documentaries running on a loop on television screens with headphones. Although I'd heard the woman in the church the night before talking about watching the news, I suppose it hadn't occurred to me that the people of Tunnelton must have access to everything that goes on in our world, somehow through the magic of television transcending the two worlds, but we didn't hear anything about them. And all they seemed to get was bad news, in comparison to their perfect world, ours must just look ridiculously depressing.

I followed the green arrows into the next room, which was almost identical but alternatively contained a wall of photographs of those who had survived the two World Wars, along with their thanks and their memories. I could see now how important this was and how often this aspect had been missed out.

When we remember those who have died fighting for their country, let us not forget those who have ever since lived with the memory of surviving.

The next smaller room depicted kings and queens, those in the monarchy that had been betrayed, scorned and beheaded, and the biographies of those who had been admired, respected and welcomed to the throne.

The reverse side to this was also displayed in full detail and colour, of course - freedom, happiness, the independence of countries, and the end of rationing, of the recession, and of waiting for the wars to cease. Film stars were born. Televisions, telephones, central heating, cars, trains, planes, computers and electricity were invented. Every invention that had ever been recorded was listed, from sliced bread to space stations.

Always look on the bright side of life.

There were jobs, there were houses, and there was a man on the moon. There was the theatre, the musicals, the swinging sixties and The Beatles. There was love, there was life, and there was Elvis. There were package holidays and there was convenience food. There was a baby boom, there was an industrial boom. There was liberation and damage limitation. There was always a reason to go on.

There's always a light at the end of the tunnel.

As I approached the last few displays of the museum a small group of people were catching up with me. I detoured slightly off the green arrow route and slipped into one of the quiet reading rooms that were down the corridor leading back to the entrance hall.

The room contained just one small, freestanding bookcase but it was full to breaking point with history books, and there was a wooden desk and chair in the centre of the room. I picked up a selection of the books, piled them up on the desk and nipped out for a complimentary coffee from the machine I had spotted a little further down the corridor.

I sat staring for half an hour at the first book I had opened, never managing to read past the first line. My head was resting in my left hand, my plastic cup of coffee in my right. I wasn't feeling sad or homesick, and I'd only been up for a few hours so I couldn't have been tired. I think I just felt exhausted by everything I'd learnt, everything I'd been told over the last few days, even just today. It was New Year's Day, the start of a whole new year, but my life was no longer as I knew it. I was away from home, not voluntarily, but not by force either. I was being shown so much. I was learning more about this town and its values every minute, but what was it all for? Should I be making notes? Or going home to face irrational questions with rational answers? Or was it all just trying to teach me something? Something I was doing wrong, something I had been misunderstanding all these years?

11
Screensaver

All that thinking had left me hungry again, so I left the museum by the back door rather than retracing my steps across the rope bridge, therefore avoiding another walk through the park. This got me back on track to the town centre where I enjoyed an egg and mushroom-filled crêpe, sitting on a bench watching the street entertainers. The town centre was much busier than I'd seen it before and there was no sign of a holiday for New Year's Day there either. It was nice though, it reminded me of Covent Garden, although of course it wasn't quite *that* busy. There were magicians, buskers playing accordions, children laughing at a Punch and Judy show, a mime artist and a man playing a saw!

The setting for the scene, and by that I mean the old-fashioned shops, the roads and the buildings were still very dull and brown, but the atmosphere was much more colourful than I remembered it: the entertainers' outfits, the bright blue sky and the children's laughter.

When I'd finished eating I bravely entered a clothes shop. I had been in Tunnelton for nearly five days by this time and had only washed my clothes once in the motel. I had started to feel quite dirty, although I had managed to have a shower that morning in the hostel; it was worth a try I thought.

The shop I chose was as different from the professional tailors as I could find. It sold sportswear, suits off the rack and did dry-cleaning and alterations. It was a family-run business. I knew this first of all because it said so on the shop sign: 'Family-run since 1687'. I'm assuming not by the same members of the family but you never know do you? And secondly by the greeting I received when I entered the shop.

'Good afternoon sir, how may we help you?' rang out in stereo from Mr and Mrs Stitch. Those weren't their real names, but as I never asked them what their names were, for the purpose of this story they are Mr and Mrs Stitch, like in the Happy Families card game!

I've never seen a shop assistant so happy to assist in all my life. Mrs Stitch removed my denim jacket and sent it off on an electric rail to the dry-cleaning room, and then I complied with their request to hand over my shoes. They simultaneously passed me vacuum-packed shirts and trousers, freshly ironed tracksuit bottoms, T-shirts (without embarrassing logos this time), multi-coloured socks and boxer shorts on a coat hanger!

Then they pointed me towards the dressing room, a very spacious, pentagonal-shaped room with ceiling-to-floor mirrors on every side. Not really what anyone wants to see - their body from every possible angle - and what had happened to my hair?!

I didn't try on everything they had given me, I just chose what I liked and left everything else neatly in its packet. I emerged from the dressing room to almost 'proud-parent' looking faces as I stood there in the tracksuit bottoms and polo shirt (and clean underwear!) Mr Stitch passed me my trainers, now as good as new - the white was white, the blue was blue, the soles were clean and they had new laces in them - then Mrs Stitch held out my clean denim jacket for me to put on. She then gathered together all my own clothes that I had taken off and put them in a wicker basket that was sent down the electric rail.

'How do I pay you for all this?' I asked.

Mr and Mrs Stitch looked at each other and with a tilt of

their heads smiled back at me.

'Don't worry about it,' Mrs Stitch said, 'we won't.'

'You'll get your clothes back when you leave Tunnelton,' Mr Stitch continued.

'And we'll get ours back,' Mrs Stitch interjected as they continued to alternate speaking parts.

I smiled, confused but quite satisfied with the arrangement.

'Give and take,' Mr Stitch said, almost singing now. 'It's just an illusion, this new found obsession with image.'

'Vanity,' Mrs Stitch added.

'You could walk around here in a spacesuit.'

'In fancy dress.'

'In your pyjamas,' they both laughed, 'and no one would blink an eye.'

'You probably think it's old-fashioned, the way we dress, don't you?'

'Well it's kind of an old-fashioned place for the most part,' I stuttered, not wanting to cause offence.

'But nobody pays any attention to detail like that you see.' Mr Stitch was talking and sewing a button on a shirt at the same time. 'It's just a mask, a disguise, until you let someone past that, let someone into your mind.'

'It's like a screensaver,' Mrs Stitch went on. 'It's just there so as not to expose the inside to anyone you don't want to show it to.'

'Then you need a password.'

A password? This took me back to the mystery of the human safe and, in fact, my whole existence in Tunnelton. Was it like one huge computer program that I had accidentally hacked into? Passwords and codes, it all seemed to be getting very complicated.

'Not a password like a word or an eight-digit number,' Mrs

Stitch explained correcting my thoughts.

'Oh no,' Mr Stitch agreed, 'nothing like that, more like eye contact, interest, friendship or the most powerful of course, love.'

At this the old couple smiled at each other fondly. 'Then they no longer see the clothes, the screensaver hovering there, they see what's behind it.'

'But for now we know you'll feel better in clean clothes so you just hurry along on your way and we'll swap everything back when you check out,' Mrs Stitch told me.

'When you log off!' This was Mr Stitchs' joke, which had them both, for several minutes in, well, stitches! I turned and walked out of the shop in my new disguise.

12
Organised Time

I didn't have a specific destination in mind for the afternoon or evening of this very unique New Year's Day, so I strolled around the town centre for a bit longer looking for the next chapter of Tunnelton madness to attract my attention.

As I mentioned before, my watch hadn't been working properly since I'd arrived. It hadn't actually stopped completely, it just seemed to slow down and then speed up at random intervals. At first I took this in my stride, thinking it must be somehow related to the Daylight-Saving theory, and as I couldn't rely on the sun, due to this very reason, to tell me when it was night and day, I had been living pretty much by my body clock; eating when I was hungry, sleeping when I was tired, shopping and exploring anywhere and at any time I could!

Anyway, there was a street vendor I had noticed earlier who sold and mended watches and clocks. He worked out of a kind of metal caravan, the kind you would see selling chips or candyfloss at the fair. I thought this was worth a try, and anyway, if he couldn't help me I was sure the conversation would enlighten me somehow. The Tunneltonians had never yet disappointed me.

When I reached the counter, which was almost too high for me to see over, the man was looking at the inside of a miniature grandfather clock with a magnifying glass.

'Hello' I said cheerily.

The man silently finished off the job he was doing, put the clock aside and came forward to sit on a stool located behind the counter.

'I wondered if you could have a look at my watch please,' I continued politely. The man was probably not much older than me, anything up to about thirty I guess, but he didn't seem to care much about his appearance and therefore looked a lot older. He was very thin with collar-length, straggly brown hair, he was unshaven, he had been wearing the same clothes for longer than I had before my visit to Mr and Mrs Stitch's, and he had a ring in his nose and several more in both ears. He looked like a Dickens character, and he was a man of very few words.

'Broken?' is all he asked.

'Yes' I replied.

'Stopped?'

'Well no, but...'

'Fast and slow?'

'Yes,' I answered in wonder at his correct diagnosis.

'Follow me.'

The man opened a hatch by the side of him and I climbed under the counter into the caravan. There wasn't much there apart from his tools, the few clocks and watches he had been left to fix and a few more new ones in a desk-top glass display case. Then he kneeled down, opened another hatch on the floor and started climbing down underground. He didn't give me any further instructions so I waited until he was out of sight then followed him. There was a ladder that took you down, out of the bottom of the caravan and into a basement in the ground. My feet finally touched the floor and I had a look around to see just where he was taking me. The room was more or less the same size as the caravan, which was quite big for an underground den, and although when climbing down the ladder I thought I would be going down into the sewers or somewhere dingy and dirty, this place was actually cleaner than the caravan itself. The room was made of studded aluminium sheets that encased you in a kind of workshop that was a cross between a bomb shelter and the inside of a rocket. Spotlights were fitted in the ceiling, reflecting light off the walls and giving the room its post modern, minimalist look.

The only furniture I could see was an aluminium chair that was bolted to the middle of the floor, a couple of tall metal stools like the one upstairs and a computer stand housing the world's smallest laptop. The man was standing by a projector that hung on a bracket off the far wall.

'Sit,' he instructed, then came over to me, held out his hand and said, 'Watch.'

Now I know it sounds like he was being rude and unfriendly but really he was just quiet. And if you read on you'll see that he actually turned out to be quite nice.

He took my watch and, after unscrewing the lid off the top of the projector, placed it in a custom-made watch-holder inside. Then he pulled down a white screen from a pole on the ceiling, turned off the lights and switched on the projector. The first screen that came up was a pretty ordinary computer log-on screen.

Under 'username' he typed Sebastian, which I assumed to be his name.

'Name?' he then asked me.

'Paddy,' I replied, which he must have typed in at the password prompt.

Some music began playing out of surround-sound speakers, then the screen took on a personality of its own, flashing through the colours of the rainbow before settling on blue. On the blue background image appeared a childlike drawing of a clock face and several more question and answer fields within a pop-up window.

'Date of birth?' Sebastian asked.

'21st of December 1980,' I replied and he typed in 21/12/80.

'House number?'

'Six.'

'Telephone number? Parents' house number? Year of graduation?'

All of these questions I answered in the same digital monotone in which they were asked, and he tapped the answers into the laptop computer.

Then the film started, although it wasn't very interesting. Images appeared on the screen at random, but they didn't mean anything to me; they didn't give me flashbacks of my life so far or include messages from my worried family and friends. They were just like postcard pictures of cities, which I may or may not have visited, and they came and went so quickly I couldn't recognise them, together with computer images of graphs and charts - boring stuff!

When the screen returned to the blue background with the clock face, the music stopped and the lights came back on. Sebastian pulled up a stool next to me and held on to my watch as we talked. When he talked in full sentences he actually sounded quite timid and he very rarely looked me in the eye, choosing instead to stare at my watch or the now uneventful projector screen.

'You've been reset' was the first thing Sebastian said to me, as if it was an everyday occurrence and nothing to worry about.

'Okay,' I replied, hoping he would continue with an explanation for his statement.

'It's just a glitch,' he went on. 'Your time gets shuffled around when you come here. It gets confused and ends up disorganised, but it's okay now.'

'Oh good,' I nodded, but I couldn't get my head round this one at all.

He gave my watch one last tap with his finger before passing it back to me, then thankfully he started talking again.

'Time is like a game of mathematics. It has very strict rules and right and wrong answers with nothing in between. It doesn't like to be questioned or confused. It has a routine and it likes to stick to it. You will understand more when you leave.'

'That's what people keep saying,' I explained, 'but I have no idea when that will be.'

'No, of course. I understand that must be worrying for you.'

'Well I wouldn't exactly say I was worried, just very confused.'

'Confused, yes, you will be.' Sebastian spoke in his quiet drawl as if each answer had required a careful calculation in his head, and he never laughed. He was almost robotic.

'Do you know why I'm here?' I asked him, thinking that he was just as likely to know the answer as anyone.

After a short pause and a quick intake of breath he replied 'No.'

'Okay, do you know how I can get home?' I tried.

'No.'

'Or how long I might be staying here for?'

'Yes,' he replied to this. I looked up anxiously but he didn't speak.

'Well?' I urged him on.

'Seven days,' he said, 'always seven full days.'

'Oh,' I replied, wondering whether as I'd already been there for four full days that meant I only had three days left. 'Do you mean seven days in total, from the evening I got here?'

'Yes.'

So, I was more than halfway through my stay, if Sebastian was right.

With this, he stood up and started to make his way back up to the ground floor so, yet again, I followed him. I was about to climb back under the counter, say my thanks and leave him to his seized cogs and broken second hands but he turned back towards me after switching on a kettle and asked, 'Tea?'

'Oh, yes please,' I replied, unsure of what he wanted the answer to be.

'Sugar?' he asked as he pointed to another stool tucked under the counter for me to sit on.

'No, thanks.'

He stood facing away from me until the kettle had boiled and the tea had been made, but then he came over, passed me the large mug of tea and sat down next to me.

'It's a bit like the Theory of Relativity,' Sebastian began, in his robotic, monotone voice. 'You know the Michelson-Morley experiment, the failure of Newtonian mechanics, Galileo's Principle of Relativity, leading on to Einstein's Theory of Relativity and, just as importantly, his Relativity of Simultaneity?'

'Well, not in any great detail,' I replied, wondering for a second whether he was intentionally trying to make me feel stupid. Sebastian put down his cup of tea, started playing with the frayed ends of his jumper sleeves, and without looking up at me continued.

'Is the train moving or is the platform moving? Are space and time intervals absolute and the speed of light relative or is the speed of light absolute and space and time intervals relative? Was Newton correct or was Einstein correct?'

I looked up at him, not sure if the pause meant he was actually waiting for me to answer, but he was still looking down at his knees so I drank my tea and waited to hear something that made sense.

'Should we adopt Descartes' Method of Doubt, choosing not to trust the instincts that come naturally to us, believing that everything we've ever learnt or been told could be a lie, one huge deception on the part of an evil demon acting as a God substitute? Should we take on Aurelius' elegant optimism, appreciating the useful pieces of knowledge and virtues that we pick up on our journey through life? Should we only believe what has been proven and look rather to the mathematicians and physicists for the truth? Or should we share Montaigne's motto, shrug our shoulders and think "What do I know?"'

With this, Sebastian lifted his head and smiled. Now he was waiting for me to answer.

'I'm afraid I don't know,' I replied. 'It's all very interesting but I can't claim to understand it, and I can't really see its relevance to my current situation.'

Sebastian laughed, he actually laughed, probably at me but nevertheless I was much more fond of him after that.

'It's got everything to do with your current situation,' he exclaimed, making me pay a little more attention. 'Your watch was working until you came here wasn't it?' I nodded. 'Then it tried to change to fit in with our time. You thought it was broken when in fact it just needed resetting to fit in. So whose is correct, yours or ours? To you, your world of Hepby, in Yorkshire, in England, in the world, in the galaxy is real and Tunnelton is surreal. If you weren't awake you'd think it was a dream. But how do you know you're awake? Our world of Tunnelton is real and your world of Hepby, North Yorkshire, England is surreal to us. We know it's there because people come here and tell us it's there, but how do we really know? And can our world and your world be running simultaneously yet never cross paths?'

I was speechless. I shook my head to answer, 'I don't know.'

'No,' Sebastian replied, 'and that's the beauty of it. Everything is relative. Don't waste your time always looking for an answer when you're not even sure what the question is. Time doesn't like to be wasted.'

I laughed politely and got up to leave.

'You've read *Alice in Wonderland* haven't you Paddy?' he asked finally.

'Well, I'm sure I have, a long time ago,' I answered.

'Keep on good terms with time and he'll do anything for you. That's how we get round our Daylight-Saving problem; we ask nicely!'

13
Musical Madness

After my philosophical-mathematical science lesson with Sebastian, I crashed out, completely exhausted, in a room above a music shop called 'Acciaccatura'. I didn't take much notice of the shop itself the night before, only of the sign in its window that read 'Rooms To Let'. I spoke to the woman inside, who introduced herself as Dorian, and explained that as I believed I would be in town for the next three days at least, that I would like a room until Sunday. She was very friendly. She gave me a key to the room and another key to a shared kitchen, telling me to make myself at home and to call in to see her in the shop anytime. This is what I liked about Tunnelton - everything was so simple; maybe not so simple to understand all the time, but simple when you wanted simple. There was none of this booking a hotel ten days in advance, with extras added on for room service, or if you drank the contents of the mini-bar and had forgotten all about it the morning after. Here you just looked out for the 'Vacancies' sign, helped out by enriching someone's life with the donation of a story, a picture, or just polite conversation - they didn't mind which - and you treated people how you would expect to be treated.

In the morning I went downstairs to the shop to see Dorian. We hadn't spoken much the night before; she had customers in the shop, which seemed to be open pretty much all of the time, and I had been tired, a little drained of my usual social etiquette. Dorian was, in the nicest possible way, absolutely mad. It took ten minutes for me to get a word in, between her bursts of arias, as she was dancing around the shiny stainless steel espresso-maker behind the counter. If she wasn't high on life, she was definitely high on caffeine! Dorian was an ageless, eccentric, slightly overweight music fanatic. The shop, on first impressions, appeared to sell musical instruments with a bit of sheet music and a few CDs thrown in to round it off. This, however, wasn't an entirely precise observation, but I'll go into that later.

'Hello,' I shouted out.

'Hello,' Dorian sang back at me.

'I thought I'd call in to see what it is you do down here.'

Dorian danced the waltz over to me with her invisible partner. 'Oh Paddy,' she said, flinging her arms around me, 'how lovely it is to see you again.'

'Well thank you,' I replied. 'It's a lovely room you've given me.'

'My pleasure sweetheart,' she smiled. It was at this point I noticed the faint Irish twang in her voice.

I started to have a look around the shop. It was quite dark and dusty in there as were all the other shops in town I suppose, but it certainly had an impressive collection of commodities.

Dorian saw me having a nosy around, and came to show me the instruments herself. It was on closer inspection and with the help of Dorian's insight that I noticed that none of the instruments were actually complete. It was like a 'spare parts' shop.

'What do you sell then?' I asked her. 'Instruments or just bits of instruments?'

'Bits of instruments!' she laughed. 'What sort of a phrase is that?'

'Well, you know,' I tried to explain, 'parts of instruments, spare parts.'

'Yes Paddy,' she was mocking me, 'spare parts.'

Dorian looked at me with a deadly serious expression for a couple of seconds and then she burst out laughing. She took hold of my hand and led me to the front of the shop, to the parts that were in the shop window. Lined up on the carpet-covered bay windowsill were mouthpieces of every description. There was a row of trumpet mouthpieces - this was the largest collection, then rows and rows of mouthpieces for tubas, euphoniums, saxophones, clarinets, flutes and piccolos with extra reeds for the clarinets and saxophones in labelled boxes next to them and an extra large box of bassoon reeds.

Over to the next display: to the left of the window there was a wooden filing cabinet that held every make and model of guitar, violin, viola, cello and double-bass string you could ever wish for, filed in alphabetical order. On top of that was a catalogue showing all the drum skins that could be made to order. Moving on, there were bows for every stringed instrument hung on the wall. There were trombone slides in tenor and bass sizes, pedals for bass drums lined up on the floor and a framed display of violin chin rests. By the counter, where Dorian ended the circular tour, was a box of piano keys, individual black and white ones, for replacing lost or broken keys or restoring yellowed antique pianos. Dorian was very pleased with this idea, which she'd had after her beloved baby grand piano had been damaged in a house move, but not as pleased as she was with her collection of chanters.

'Now do you know what a chanter is Paddy?' she asked.

'Erm...' I looked up at the glass case.

Dorian left me for a minute to retrieve from the back office...bagpipes!

'Now then Paddy, I know you know what these are.'

'Yes,' I smiled, 'bagpipes.'

'That's right, bagpipes. And this pipe here,' she said pointing to the pipe with the finger holes, 'this is the reed pipe, the chanter.'

'Oh okay,' I said as she began to blow into the bagpipes, stopping every few seconds as she thought of something else to say.

'On the chanter you make the melody, Paddy, do you see?'

I nodded, and then, yes, she began to play the bagpipes. I listened with a contrived smile for what seemed like hours as Dorian took to her, slightly confused, Celtic roots and danced around the room, kicking together her heels in celebration of her favourite instrument.

'Aren't you Irish?' I asked when she paused for breath. 'I mean I know you're from Tunnelton, but wouldn't your ancestors have been Irish? Or do you just pick any accent you want around here? How come you got into the bagpipes, the most traditional Scottish instrument?'

'Paddy,' she said, 'have you ever tried to play the bodhràn and the blues harp at the same time?'

'No,' I answered, trying not to laugh.

'Well then,' she said as she put down the bagpipes and returned to her coffee machine behind the counter. 'And,' she swung round, 'you're called Paddy and you're about as Irish as my Aunt Tilly, and she was a Russian spy.'

'Fair enough,' I shrugged and we both laughed.

'Now then Paddy, I don't want to keep you, no doubt you've got a busy day planned.'

'Not really,' I said.

'But Paddy,' she cried out, 'it's Friday, pet, you must follow the rain.'

I looked out of the shop window at the blue sky and dry streets.

'Follow the...'

'The rain, that's right. Now run along.' Dorian handed me one of her business cards from behind the counter. 'Ring me if you need anything at all during your stay.'

'Thank you,' I replied as I read the card. 'Dorian Mode - Acciacatura - For All Your Musical Needs'.

'Dorian Mode?' I asked before she could return to her caffeine fix. 'Isn't that some sort of scale?'

'A scale, yes,' she replied nonchalantly, 'ascending on the white notes, starting at D.'

'Oh.'

'And yes, it's my real name,' she smiled. 'My mother was from a very musical family, sort of an in-joke. Like my brother Cantando, who, faithful to his name, is always singing. And I bet you think *I* won't shut up!'

I laughed and then waved goodbye, the business card and my sanity just about intact as I began my search for the elusive rain.

14
The Umbrella Graveyard

It wasn't raining. I walked along the high street browsing in the shop windows, thinking that maybe if I waited long enough the clouds would arrive, bringing with them this downpour of rain that I was apparently waiting for. It got to four o'clock (Tunnelton Time) and I was sat in the town square watching a magnified game of chess being played with oversized pawns, wondering whether I should return to my room and give up on this inconsiderate afternoon sun. I had been wandering round, passing the time, yet I didn't know why or where I should be looking for the rain.

I stood up from the bench I had become almost stuck to in the heat, and without looking in my rear-view mirror, I mean without looking behind me, accidentally walked right into someone's path. The old man in question coughed and apologised as I did the same. Then he swung his walking stick round 360 degrees and stopped dead in his tracks.

'Well, I never,' he cried out, very loudly.

I smiled, a little embarrassed by the unwanted attention.

'If it isn't little Paddy Jones.'

Oh God, he knew my name. He knew me and I didn't know him. What should I say? What should I do? But before I could speak he continued.

'Paddy Jones. I'd know that face anywhere. You don't know who I am do you?'

I shook my head.

'That's okay my son,' he said putting his arm around me, 'there's no reason why you should. I'm Alfred. I'm an old friend of the family.'

I reached out to shake his hand. 'No, I don't recognise you, sorry.'

'Don't be sorry boy,' he replied. 'You couldn't recognise me. I was your great-great grandfather's best friend.'

'Oh.' What could you say to that? 'But you're...'

'Ha' he laughed. 'I'm not dead, no. I'm here. I've moved on. Tell me you wouldn't choose Tunnelton over Hepby any day?'

'Well, I...'

'Come on now Paddy. Your old great granddaddy had an imagination on him, give me a bit of something to go on here.'

'Oh I've got imagination,' I assured him, 'I'm just a bit...'

'Lost?'

'Yeah.'

'I know Paddy, but our paths have met. Do you believe in fate?'

'I'm starting to believe in just about everything,' I replied.

'Well then son,' he said, 'follow me.'

We walked together over to a milliner's shop on the left-hand side of the high street. At the side of the shop was a gate, and through the gate was a garden.

'Follow me,' Alfred kept saying, so I did.

The garden was just a regular-sized piece of land round the back of the shop. It was owned, I was informed, by Elise McMahon, the woman responsible for Tunnelton's dress code! Despite that, it was a beautiful garden, lined with a rockery and housing a young pine tree.

There was a low wall at the bottom of the garden, which I stepped over, following Alfred's rather practised stumble, on the other side of which was a public shortcut, a footpath. Or was it?

Alfred put out his hand to stop me before I got a footstep away from the wall. The 'Other Side' he explained was not real.

'Stay where you are Paddy,' Alfred instructed me, strictly but kindly. 'Just watch.'

So I watched this life-size cinema screen silently as Alfred stood next to me. It wasn't like the projector screen I had seen in Sebastian's basement, it was like the fake wall on a film set that makes you believe they are racing sports cars across a Nevada desert or sitting on a beach looking out over miles and miles of crashing waves when really it's just an illusion so huge that you can't see where it begins and where it ends.

'It's so sad,' he said.

'What is?' I asked.

'Look closely Paddy.'

I looked as closely at the picture as I could. And it started to rain. Spots of drizzle quickly turned into a powerful downpour. Alfred and I weren't getting wet; we were still standing underneath the Tunnelton sun, looking out onto this three-dimensional show.

As the rain got heavier, more and more people started appearing in the picture. They were mostly businessmen and women who looked like they were on their way to work, a little angry that their smart suits, their smart reputations and their smart images had been so easily ruined by a little rainwater.

The first person we saw commit the crime was a woman in a grey skirt suit and short waterproof jacket. She was struggling to keep hold of her handbag, the white scarf around her neck and her umbrella all at the same time. And then it happened. A strong gust of wind swept along the ground and back up into the sky, nearly knocking the woman off her feet and turning the umbrella inside out. The woman, in her aggravated frustration with this unsuccessful walk to work, threw the umbrella down on the ground, kicked it a few times, then stomped off, her hair, her clothes and her patience now completely ruined for the day.

The second offender was a man in a very expensive-looking suit who was attempting to make the short distance from his car to his office at the other side of the walkway without an overcoat. He had a large golfing umbrella, which he first of all carried as a walking stick until he gave up on his tough, not-caring-about-getting-wet act, and held it in the correct way, above his head. But the wind was not forgiving today; it was angry and violent and multi-directional, and it not only blew the man's umbrella inside out but it also managed to tear one or two of the coloured triangles. Alfred and I stood there watching the man lose his cool and fight with the umbrella as if it were a fully grown vicious dog, but this caused the handle to snap off so he abandoned it in the nearest bin.

Then along came the little girl, who walked innocently into this trap, this walkway of sin. She was walking alongside her mother, who was elegantly wrapped up in a long winter coat with a hood, thick woolly scarf and leather gloves. The girl was skipping along, only about waist-height to her mother. She was protected from the rain by an oversized, waterproof, yellow hooded coat, which drowned her more than the rain ever could. She had a small plastic pink children's umbrella, which she swung around more than she held it above her head. There wasn't much chance of her getting wet in that coat, so the umbrella was really just an accessory, confirming that she was well on her way to following in her mother's footsteps.

The wind and the rain worked together to claim their next

victim: the plastic pink umbrella. It shot up into the air like an escaping helium balloon, and five seconds later came crashing down at the little girl's feet.

'Mum!' she cried helplessly as she stamped her foot in a muddy puddle on the ground. The woman took hold of her daughter's hand and pulled her, sulking, along the footpath.

I looked over to Alfred whose eyes were still firmly fixed on the scene. We watched for a little while longer as the same scenario kept repeating itself with different actors, except they weren't actors; these were real people going about their real lives and we were watching them like animals in a zoo, for research purposes.

'So where is this place?' I asked Alfred, bringing him out of his trance.

'It's just outside London,' he replied. 'I'm not entirely sure as it's a different place each week.'

'Oh. And is it always raining?' I asked.

'It's always raining somewhere at 4.30 on a Friday afternoon,' he explained, and turning around to point to the back wall of the milliner's shop he continued, 'That window there seeks out the rain and, just like a web cam, lets us watch other people's lives for ten minutes once a week to see if we can solve this terrible dilemma.'

'The dilemma of what?' I asked, although I thought I knew what he meant. I thought he meant the dilemma of the bad weather that appeared to be taking over the world, but I had also learnt not to jump to conclusions.

'The dilemma, Paddy' he said turning back to face me, 'of all the dead umbrellas.' He took my frown as a cue to continue. 'It's so very sad.' He was getting quite emotional now. 'Look at all those umbrellas, twenty or so have ended up on the ground already and the rain has only been falling for ten minutes. They are discarded by their owners because they haven't been able to do their job properly, so they're made redundant, sent home for bad behaviour, beaten up by the wind and then left to die.' Alfred wiped away a tear with the back of his hand.

'I didn't think umbrellas had feelings,' I commented, trying my best at a little compassion but not really understanding what the big deal was about.

'Well Paddy, that's where you're wrong,' he went on. 'Umbrellas come into the world with a purpose. For months they might be thrown to the back of a cloakroom, or underneath a shoe rack, or in the boot of a car, but when the rain comes out they are celebrated. People are excited and relieved when they realise they have got one ready to use, ready to protect them from the unpredictable weather. But if they fail, Paddy,' he shook his head in disgust, 'if they dare to fail just the once, they're not ever given a second chance.'

'I'm sorry, I didn't realise.'

'It's not your fault Paddy,' Alfred said patting my back, 'no one does. Let me take you to the umbrella graveyard and then it might make a little more sense. I was going myself anyway. I visit every Friday.'

If you're wondering whether it occurred to me that I was in the presence of a madman masquerading as an old family friend, then yes I did, but I had to follow him didn't I? I couldn't have left the story unfinished.

To get to the umbrella graveyard we had to walk through the illusion of the city walkway that had now come to the end of its weekly show and now showed just a still image of the path, without its actors, weather machine and props; I'm so cynical! Alfred told me that it might feel a bit strange; a bit like you're a ghost walking through a door for the first time, but he promised me it would be worth the trip. I followed as Alfred led the way further into the field. To be perfectly honest, I didn't feel much at all when we walked through the projected image, maybe a bit of a change in temperature, but nothing too painful, and we emerged at the other side of the field which, at first sight, didn't strike me as being any different to where we had just been standing.

I expected to see, at the umbrella graveyard, judging from its name, pieces of torn cloth poking out from behind tombstones, and flowers being set down on the ground, condolence cards sellotaped to them. But it was nothing like that.

The umbrella graveyard was, for a start, mostly indoors, but it was also as far from one's usual perception of a graveyard as is possible. We walked down to the bottom of the sloping field eventually entering a valley, and over the hill, where I hadn't been able to see before, was a large, sturdy shed. Although its walls were made of stone, it had a pointed roof and two large swinging wooden doors to the front. I suppose it was more of a detached garage than a shed, but it was standing there on its own, its sole purpose to protect this unusual graveyard from a multitude of weathers.

When we arrived at the shed, Alfred knocked on the door. It took a few minutes to get a response, in which time the sun had gone down, leaving us, now shivering a little, in the dusk.

Both doors opened smoothly and slowly and simultaneously, so much so that if you had been anywhere else but Tunnelton you would have known that they were automatic doors, or at least operated by some kind of electronic system, but this was Tunnelton, and the reason why these doors opened that way was because they were being pulled open by 92-year-old twins that ran The Umbrella Graveyard; twins who did and said everything at exactly the same time.

The shed had been fitted out like someone's workshop, but by someone who intended spending more time in it than in their own house. It was carpeted and wallpapered and contained two easy chairs, a sink and two identical workbenches. The twins wore blue and white lumberjack shirts and brown corduroy overalls. They were very thin and the single fluff of white hair that they both owned stood upwards in the centre of their heads like antennae.

'Hello,' they greeted us, waving their left hands in the air.

Alfred shook their hands, one after the other and I stood back, waiting to be spoken to.

'I'm Neville,' said one of them to me. 'He's Neville,' said the other one at the same time.

'He's Tobias,' said Neville. 'I'm Tobias,' said Tobias simultaneously.

'Pleased to meet you,' I smiled.

Alfred gestured for me to enter the shed, as Neville and Tobias made some room on the bench for me to sit down. It was quite a low, waist-high workbench, so just the right height to sit and have a tea break on. I sat there, swinging my legs like a little kid and listening to the conversation between my three new friends as Alfred leaned casually against the bench next to me.

'How has this week been for you boys then?' Alfred asked the twins.

'Picking up a bit,' they replied.

'Have you had a lot in?' he continued.

'Yes, but we've cleared most of it away now, ready for the weekend,' the twins told him.

'I was hoping you'd be able to show young Paddy here some of your work.'

'Oh yes,' they said, jumping off the bench with much more energy than you would expect them to have.

The twins took me to the back of the workshop, which they explained was where the majority of the work was carried out. There was nothing on display, but I soon realised that the twins were very tidy and efficient and that everything had already been put away in its place. They opened a large wardrobe, again by pulling back one door each, and I looked inside in astonishment.

'These are the ones they've managed to mend,' Alfred explained to me in his most caring voice.

'These are the ones we've saved,' the twins confirmed.

So it seemed to me more like an umbrella hospital than a graveyard. The brightly coloured umbrellas were neatly hung on the clothes rail side by side, their cloth had been stitched, their handles mended and their broken spokes replaced. Neville and Tobias were clearly very fond of their job and very proud of their success as they stood there smiling the same smile whilst I had a closer look in the wardrobe.

'We get most of these sent in,' Alfred continued to speak on the twins' behalf, 'a bit like the lost property gets sent in.'

'Oh right,' I nodded.

'But of course people don't just stop and pick up a broken umbrella, they don't realise that there is something they can do to help with this tragedy.'

'They probably don't realise it's such a tragedy' I said, trying not to sound too condescending.

'No,' Alfred sighed, 'it's lucky we've got some people out there helping us to collect them or else we'd lose even more every year.'

'So what happens to the ones that can't be...saved?' I asked, and as I heard myself asking such a ridiculous question I almost lost my cool and laughed at this most peculiar charity case. Alfred, Neville and Tobias, however, took my question very seriously and you could have heard a pin drop in the silence that lasted until one of them decided to speak. Or in this case two of them because it was the twins who eventually answered my question.

'Come outside,' they told me, 'to the graveyard.'

So there was a graveyard there and we got to it by exiting the shed through a back door. This brought us out into another, very large garden. There was a row of flowers that ran around the outside of this enormous piece of land and more rows of flowers, plants and small trees running in neatly dug-out lines horizontally across the garden. So for my next question!

'Where are they then?' I asked my three guides.

'The umbrellas?' It was Alfred who asked the obvious question, his mind somewhat detached from me by this time.

'They are buried where the flowers grow,' the twins told me. 'They pass on their vibrant colours to the newborn buds and over time a flower grows for each umbrella buried.'

It was starting to sound like quite a sensible thing to do now, a worthwhile job to have. Maybe that was my cue to leave.

Neville and Tobias walked Alfred and me back to the front door. I thanked them for letting us visit and they said to come back anytime; except on a Monday because that was when the influx of injured new arrivals were delivered and it might upset me too much!

Alfred showed me the way back to the high street, then he shook my hand and let me get on my way back to my room. I still don't know whether I believe he was who he said he was, but, all things considered, I suppose it doesn't really matter does it?

15
Made to Measure

Saturday morning arrived and there was not a cloud in the sky. I called in to say hello to Dorian as I headed back out onto the high street. It was on Dorian's recommendation that I paid a visit to a psychic, which is not something I would normally be interested in. In fact I would go as far as to say that I'm very sceptical about these things, but, as my mind had surely already been stretched to its limit during my stay, what harm could an old hippy do to me? Oh how naive I can be!

Claris worked out of a little office at the back of the cobbler's. The reason for this was that she was married to Clarence, the cobbler. Claris and Clarence Cash of C. Cash & Sons Cobblers were often, I was informed by my trusted source, Dorian, the talk of the town. Their three sons, Christopher, Colin and Calum, although they were acknowledged as part of the family business on the shop sign, had now, all in their twenties, decided to go their own way. This left Clarence to do the cobbling and Claris to take care of the town's clairvoyance needs. Together they heard all the town's gossip, fixed all the town's shoes and answered all the town's questions about the dead.

I entered the cobbler's shop and politely had a browse round at the display of soles, heels, shoelaces and polish before I asked if Claris was available.

'I bet Mrs Mode's sent you hasn't she?' Clarence laughed, reaching out his hand to introduce himself. He was one of those people that, unfortunate as it is to say, you probably wouldn't recognise again. There was just nothing that immediately struck you about him, no defining features, although he seemed reasonably friendly to me, knowing full well that it wasn't him I had come to visit.

'Yes, erm, Dorian suggested that I come to see Claris,' I told him. 'It's Paddy.'

He looked blankly at me for a second then simply said, 'Go through.'

I entered the back of the shop through some strings of beads in the doorway, to find Claris sitting perfectly still at her table. It wasn't the sort of room you'd expect, not like one set up in portable, phone box-sized caravans at the seaside, with the walls covered in glittery material, mirrors and signed photos of celebrities. Instead it was just an ordinary back room, with a folding dining table and two chairs. Claris looked almost as nondescript as her husband as she sat there in blue jeans and an old black woolly jumper, with a cup of tea.

'Hello dear' she said, standing up as I entered the room. 'Can I get you a drink?'

I didn't like to ask for a large brandy so early in the morning, but that's what I felt like. I'd survived this ordeal so far without the help of being even mildly intoxicated. I hadn't seen anyone here drinking or smoking. I suppose there wasn't any need for mind-changing substances or something to help you unwind after a stressful day; there wasn't anything to be unhappy or stressed about. So I settled for a cup of tea.

Claris put the kettle on and turned off the radio that was quietly humming in the corner. I stood there feeling a bit lost as Claris made the tea, only sitting down when she did.

It was like a breath of fresh air and a weight off my shoulders to, for once, not be asked what I wanted or if I wanted a look around, and I was relieved when Claris didn't ask me if I had any questions for her. She spoke softly with a hint of a South African accent in her voice, and she told me, without any prompting, what it was that she did.

'Most people want their palms read, or to pick some tarot cards at random for me to analyse. It's all a bit boring to tell you the truth. For me, looking into a crystal ball is like having to read a book over and over again when you didn't really enjoy it the first time round. People become so predictable, they ask the same questions. What is my late husband doing now? Does my wife forgive me for shouting at her just before she died? Do you think he'll be angry if I remarry? I mean, I could do it in my sleep.'

I sat opposite Claris, holding on to my cup of tea, and listened in awe to her story. She seemed almost resentful of her gift of psychic powers, that she had no choice but to use because so many people had come to rely on her.

'Now I don't normally let people into my secrets, but for you, Paddy, I'm going to make an exception, because you're a friend of Dorian's and I know that you'll keep it to yourself. Let's face it...' she shrugged, 'who's going to believe anything you say when you get out of here!'

I forced a smile whilst frowning at the same time, not knowing quite how to take that comment.

'Let's do something different with this mind of mine today shall we Paddy?' Claris said nudging my arm. 'What do you say to a bit of a history lesson?'

'Okay,' I replied, glad that it wasn't going to be a mind-reading session, or worse.

'Did you do history at school?' Claris asked me as she slid a pack of playing cards off the worktop onto the table in front of her.

'Yes,' I replied, 'but I was never very good at it.'

'I can't believe that.' she said. 'Pass me your hand.'

I reached across the table with my right hand turned upwards.

'The other one,' she laughed. 'Have you never done this before?'

'No,' I answered, thinking that it wasn't really through any fault of my own that I was here and that I didn't know which palm she would want to read. I reluctantly slid my left hand over to her, becoming less comfortable in her presence as each minute passed.

'Oh I see,' Claris continued at she glanced at my palm whilst shuffling the cards. 'You're more creative aren't you, than academic?'

'I suppose so,' I shrugged, 'although I wouldn't say creative exactly, more...'

'Artistic,' she said proudly as if she had just plucked the word she had been looking for out of the air. I nodded nervously. 'What is it you do then Paddy?'

'Well, I'm working as an architect,' I told her.

'Of course' she replied, squinting her eyes as if she herself had drawn the answer to my lips.

'The thing about history,' Claris continued, reverting back to her chosen subject, 'is that it isn't as set in stone as you might think.'

I let her continue talking and flicking through the pack of cards without interrupting her with any questions. Well what is there to ask after such a statement?

Claris then held the cards still in front of her. These were just ordinary well-worn playing cards, not tarot cards like you might expect. She laid the first three cards of the pile face down on the table and pulled her chair up closer. Then she turned over the first card - the two of diamonds, and the third card - the four of diamonds.

'Now,' she began, putting down the rest of the cards and articulating her explanations with her hands, 'we can look at this in two ways. We can either look at it in a logical, mathematical kind of way, knowing that the obvious guess for the card in the middle would be...'

'The three of diamonds,' I answered on cue.

'Or, we can look at it the way history does; recognise that we need to get from A to B, or in this case from the two of diamonds to the four of diamonds, and think that it doesn't really matter how we do it. You see, the three of diamonds is no more likely to come up than the jack of spades is it?'

'No.'

'The laws of probability don't favour one card over another because it matches the suit we want. Or else we'd all win at poker wouldn't we?' she laughed. 'And where's the fun in that?'

I began to relax a bit more now as Claris did. She wafted her arms about whenever a bit more expression was needed, stopping every now and again to tuck her long brown hair back behind her ears where it belonged. Then, instead of turning over the mystery card in the middle, she dealt another row of three cards face down above them, and another three above them, therefore creating a three by three square of playing cards, all face down except for the revealed two of diamonds and four of diamonds.

'Turn over one card on the top row for me Paddy,' Claris instructed me.

'Any?' I asked.

'Any one you like.'

I turned over the card in the centre of the top row. It was the ten of clubs. Then Claris turned over the card to its left; the nine of clubs. Finally she turned over the third card on the middle row. It was the king of hearts.

'Your turn,' she said very quietly.

I turned over the card to the left of hers, the card in the centre of the square. It was the queen of hearts.

'Okay, now stop there,' she told me.

We sat in silence for a couple of minutes whilst Claris finished her tea and stared at the cards with her narrowed eyes.

'The easiest way to think about history,' Claris continued when she snapped out of her trance, 'is to think of it like you would a story. Now, I know the facts are very important in this case, but...' she over emphasised this point with her hands and almost sent her empty cup flying, 'there still has to be a beginning, a middle and an end for it to make any sense.'

'Yes I suppose so,' I agreed to keep her spirits up.

'Cause and effect Paddy, that's all it is.'

I tried to remember where I'd heard that before. Was it from Lorrie talking about the war museum, the way everything had to be balanced out? Maybe my pieces of knowledge were starting to come together now, forming a fuller picture.

'Imagine you were teaching a class, and in that class you had to describe to them a battle that had been fought between two enemy sides,' Claris told me.

I nodded to confirm that I was imagining it just like she said.

'So, you need to tell them how and why the battle began, what the battle consisted of, who was fighting and how long it lasted, and then finally how and why it ended.'

'Makes sense,' I said.

'Now, imagine that the history book you were learning from yourself, your source of information, told you the beginning and the middle but not the end.'

This reminded me of the library, where all the books finished before the end.

'Or, imagine that the documentary you were showing to explain this battle started in the middle of the programme, like someone had almost forgotten to record it, but then remembered just a little bit too late, giving you a middle and an end but no beginning.'

I smiled as I thought to myself that I would ask round my friends to see if anyone else had taped it, but I think we were talking hypothetically, like it was the last remaining piece of footage about that particular battle and someone had stupidly ruined it.

'Or,' I knew where she was going by now, but listened politely anyway, 'imagine you got a roll of photos developed and the processing machine chewed it up halfway through, leaving you with photographic evidence of the beginning and the end with nothing in the middle.'

Okay, so I had imagined all three of Claris' fictitious predicaments; what was her point?

Claris pointed to the still unknown card at the top right-hand corner of the square.

'If I were to change this card from the jack of clubs to the six of hearts, that wouldn't dramatically change anything in the world would it?' she asked.

'How do you know it's the jack of clubs?' I asked.

'It's the jack of clubs,' she smiled. 'By altering the record of historical events that have been kept for years, decades, sometimes centuries, we are not in any way altering the actual events that took place are we?'

I shook my head.

'We are making it easier to understand,' she went on to explain. 'By adjusting the record to fit in with our understanding, we are doing no more harm than the harm done by Chinese whispers; the human condition that cannot help adding a little of its own imagination to the truth.'

'No I suppose not,' I agreed, not really having much choice. 'So what do you do then?'

Claris turned over the card on the top right-hand corner; it was the jack of clubs just as she had said, then she turned over the card on the left of the middle row: it was the jack of hearts; and finally the card in the centre of the bottom row: the three of diamonds. This last card she picked up and played with as she answered my question.

'We fill in the gaps,' she said perfectly calmly, 'with what people expect to be there.'

She handed me the three of diamonds card, which I took to mean this was the end of my psychic session with Claris, smiled nervously at her and then her husband, as I said my goodbyes and hurried back out to the street.

16
Remote Control

It was later that same day that I noticed some strange things happening. Now I know that might sound a bit odd in light of some of the events that I had encountered over the last few days, but these were strange things that I seemed to be making happen. I decided to spend the afternoon alone rather than returning to the music shop, or my room or visiting anywhere else where I might come into contact with some more quirky characters. I had enjoyed getting to know so many of the locals and finding out so many interesting, albeit mostly unbelievable, facts about the place, but I was now starting to feel ready to go home. If Sebastian was right then this would be happening in the next couple of days, so I planned on lying low and enjoying the last of my time there in peace, even though I had no idea how it was all going to come to an end; I still didn't know how I was going to get out of there and back on track to York. However, a quiet afternoon I may have had, but an uneventful one it certainly wasn't.

It was still busy on the high street when I got back there; there was a queue at the crêpe van and a few groups of people had gathered together ready to watch the monster chess final. I passed by them and headed out of the town centre, in the direction of the park but with no real intention of making it that far. It was a nice walk away from the busy street, as it quickly turned back into countryside and very soon there was no one to be seen.

I was walking underneath the monorail track, retracing my

route from the little village. The odd car drove by and I started playing a little game to while away the time, guessing when the next monorail train would pass by me overhead by counting down from ten to its arrival. I got it right the first couple of times and thought this was just beginner's luck. Then when I got to the monorail station and the next train stopped there when I expected it to I took a guess at how many people I thought would get off the train.

'Five,' I said out loud, so as not to cheat myself. And I was right; an elderly couple, a younger couple and a young boy got off the train before it set off again, making way for the next one that arrived six minutes later, coming in the opposite direction, just as I'd predicted.

I was enjoying this game, particularly because I was doing so well at it. I wondered whether I had been doing this all along, and my meetings with people and my involvement in all things Tunnelton-related had all been carefully calculated by my subconscious. This wasn't something that I thought I could ask anyone; they would surely either think I was mad, well madder, or not understand what I meant. I decided instead to keep this little game going for the rest of the day and try to come to some sort of conclusion myself.

I did almost make it back to the park, but I certainly didn't want to wander back in there by myself again. I thought it safest to stick to the outskirts and enjoy the deserted countryside.

A new environment is very easy to adjust to; you find the first few days are so filled with curiosity and questions and things to do that, like being on holiday, you don't really think about going home or think about what it would be like if you never went home, if you ended up, by choice or otherwise, staying in a place that you were only intending to visit. That's a pretty accurate summary of what was going on in my head as I walked from the town centre to the edge of the park and back again that Saturday afternoon. I still had lots of questions, some of which no doubt would only be answered on my departure, at the same time, I was hoping, as my grip on reality would be reinstated.

The country roads were so quiet that I was surprised the sun didn't go in on the couple of occasions that I stopped for a rest. The town centre would probably be clearing by now as the afternoon drew to a close. Then I started to think about the Daylight-Saving theory again and how every person in Tunnelton had some sort of control over it; if you needed sunlight, there it was. Could the same apply to the rest of Tunnelton's services? For example the trains; every time I expected one to arrive at the station it did, as if it had been summoned by some intergalactic force. Could I change the time just as easily as Sebastian had reset it? I tried to imagine what life on Earth would be like if, instead of our working to the routine of time and the sun, they worked to ours. It's practically impossible to think along those lines, and if you start, you'll probably be deep in thought for quite some time, believe me!

So was it up to me to make my way to the exit in time for leaving? How did I know what to do? I had been living each day as it arrived. At least I think I'd been living. I suppose I could be mistaken about that too. Was this all just a dream? Was my car really lying on its back in a ditch in Hepby and I was just stuck in limbo, not quite dead like the thinkers but having not yet quite made it to Heaven, like Iris Mennison?

I suppose it could be that in the case of a world without a government and without the vast majority being particularly religious, in its traditional meaning anyway, then the ruling of the town and the way it worked was a responsibility divided evenly between its inhabitants. I still hadn't found out exactly why no one paid for anything, but I suppose this idea of 'give and take' and of everything having a counter-balance was at least starting to make a bit more sense. And in fairness it seemed to work; I hadn't seen it cause any arguments.

Could I possibly have some control over the outside world then? If the two worlds supposedly ran simultaneously, in parallel lines, how had I managed to make the jump across? Being the first person to crack the safe was a nice idea, but surely I couldn't really have been the first? Unless I was just the first since they decided they wanted a visitor; maybe they were using me to test their theories? None of it really made much sense. Although I had found the locals very friendly, I hadn't really felt, with perhaps the exception of Mrs Featherstone, and maybe Alfred if I believed his story, that I had been expected.

I tired myself out from thinking so much and I was very relieved to see the music shop come back into view. I thought, 'I bet Dorian will be waiting for me.'

Dorian was sitting in the kitchen with a brown-coloured drink that looked suspiciously like dark rum. Surely Dorian wasn't going to spoil my idea of this town being teetotal? And if she was, I hoped she would offer me some!

'Oh sit down Paddy,' Dorian said, pleased to see me. 'Can I get you a drink?'

'What are you drinking?' I asked

'It's, erm, Brown Syrup,' she mumbled.

'Is it...alcoholic?' I asked hesitantly, worried in case it was a medicinal, non-alcoholic brandy or something equally uninteresting.

'Yes,' she answered bluntly, then after a pause asked, 'would you like a glass?'

'Yes please,' I answered eagerly.

'Oh thank goodness for that,' she sighed as she got up to pour me a glass of the ... yes it was dark rum, I saw the bottle. 'I thought you were going to be disgusted for a minute there.'

'Why?' I asked, enjoying my first sip.

'It's not very popular around here,' she explained. 'Well you can imagine, there's hardly any stress is there, or really any social events for that matter. It's not frowned upon exactly, just rationed. It doesn't arrive here as easily as it does in most other places; we have to make it. We don't exactly get many deliveries of imports here.'

'No,' I said, I don't suppose you do, but it's very nice.' Dorian laughed. 'And just for the record, it's very popular where I come from!'

'Oh, I'll have to visit sometime,' Dorian smiled as we made a toast to...something!

That was the last night I spent in the room above the music shop.

17
Where the Ducks Go

When I woke up the next morning I somehow just knew that I had to make my way back to Mrs Featherstone's. That was the closest place to where I had entered Tunnelton and my instincts told me that that was probably the most likely way I would get out too. I said goodbye to Dorian as I handed in my key, and walked to the town centre monorail station with the intention of finding Deer Mountain again. That way I would know how to get back to Mrs Featherstone's, even if it did mean climbing back up that enormous mountain, or walking the long way round it, which I felt was probably more likely.

A train arrived at the platform just as I did. What a coincidence! The familiarity of the journey was comforting as we passed the town, the park, the village and arrived at the stop near to Deer Mountain where I had encountered the Iris Mennison kids.

I knew my way from there. Well, I knew in which direction I should be heading and I could see that if I just kept walking in that general direction I would eventually find myself at the other side of the mountain. I didn't know if I was in a hurry. I knew it was Sunday and so therefore I had been there a week. So was today the day? Or was I going to be spending a night under the oak tree again, or sat at Mrs Featherstone's dining table?

I tried to walk with the mountain to my left and the sun to my right. That way I knew I was heading in the right direction, but it was harder to do than I had imagined. The country roads wound in and out of the fields and I lost my coordination a couple of times. Although the deer tattoo on the mountain side was hard to miss, the path I took only gave me a view of the ever-multiplying fields on the south side that joined the steep mountain to the slow climb of the hill, which was very plain and deserted with no distinguishing marks to follow. For almost an hour I was walking in completely the opposite direction to the one intended, with my back to the mountain altogether, but it was the only way to get round the fields. I wasn't going to risk walking through the fields; I didn't know who they belonged to for a start and there were some pretty mean looking rams and bulls around!

It was on this accidental diversion that I came across the most stunning lake you could imagine. This wasn't anything like your usual village lake where small children take their mouldy bread and fishing fanatics sit for hours with a fishing rod on tiny buffets next to a tin of maggots waiting for a bite. The lake wasn't particularly big, but the sun reflected off it and leafy trees encircled it. It was so hidden away, in fact, that I hadn't even noticed it before from the top of the mountain or from the monorail train. But this runaway path that was keeping me fit in leading me back to Mrs Featherstone's house the longest way it could invent, had also led me there, and I was very glad it had.

I was relieved to sit down on the grass and take a short break from my homeward-bound trek and I was more than happy to sit and admire the view. As I was hoping I was on my way to the exit I kind of wished I had found this little gem sooner; it would have been the perfect place to camp out, had I come prepared! I sat on the soft grass with my legs stretched out in front of me, propped up on my hands whilst I admired the shimmers of sunlight that were creating waves across the lake and tried to take in the enormity of the trees that protected it from the elements, however friendly the elements may be!

It wasn't long before I noticed the shadow of a figure over on the other side of the lake. As my eyes focused in after staring so long at the bright sun, I realised it was a man sieving the lake of fallen dead leaves. He made his way over to me whilst still balancing on the edge of the lake taking care not to miss any of the wayward brown leaves. As he got closer, I wondered whether I should leave; this might be private property after all. But he didn't look unfriendly, and to be honest, he didn't look like the owner of this place and he wasn't. He was only about my age and was obviously very fond of his job at the lake; I could tell by the way he was carefully cleaning it. I decided to stay where I was and say hello to him as he passed by. But he didn't pass me by, he chose instead to come and sit on the grass next to me.

'Beautiful isn't it?' he said.

'Yes,' I agreed.

This was Eddie. And Eddie confused me just as much, if not more than, anyone else I had met in that crazy place.

'That's all I do,' he told me, quite voluntarily, 'clean the lake.'

'Oh,' I replied.

'And I love it,' he smiled. I nodded back at him and as the sun shone brighter we both sighed at the view.

'I haven't noticed this place before,' I told him.

'No, it's hidden away on purpose,' he explained. 'Well, I say on purpose, being in hiding is its purpose.'

'Its purpose for what?' I asked.

'Its purpose in life,' Eddie said.

'Which is?'

'Which is to look after the ducks.'

'The ducks?'

'The ducks.'

And, on cue, a duck and her ten tiny ducklings swam elegantly past us. Eddie nodded in affirmation of his knowledge and I'm not certain about this but I think he may have saluted them! I wanted to ask what was so special about the ducks; they were harmless creatures that made for the calmest of atmospheres at this beautiful lake, but surely the investment in a full-time lake cleaner whose job was to make the ducks as comfortable as possible was something of an overkill? Or maybe not.

'So what is this place?' I chose to ask instead.

'This is Tunnelton Lake,' Eddie said, sitting upright, 'and the home of the ducks.'

'Well, I'm glad I came across it after all.'

'Yes,' Eddie laughed, 'you should be glad. You would never have got out of here if you hadn't.'

'What do you mean? Why?' I asked. Eddie obviously knew that I'd stumbled across the lake on my way to the exit.

'It's the only rule we have here,' he continued, still laughing at my expense. 'You have to come and feed the ducks.'

'Before I can go home?'

'Yes.' And with this Eddie reached inside the large pocket to the front of his overalls and pulled out some crusts of bread. 'Here,' he whispered as he passed them to me.

I looked a little puzzled but nevertheless got up and threw them into the pond, creating a feeding frenzy amongst the little ducklings.

Eddie looked up to the sky and I did the same. It was then that I realised, before his explanation, that the centre of the lake, where the leafy branches of the trees almost, but not quite, met in the middle, was the sun.

'The sun doesn't move from this point,' Eddie told me as I sat back down again on the grass, 'or rather, as in your world, we don't move away from the sun. Tunnelton spins on its other axis so this point is always facing the sun, therefore the lake has the perfect balance of warmth and shade at all times.

'For the ducks?' I asked.

'Yes.'

We sat there in silence for a while longer before I said I was leaving to find Mrs Featherstone's house. But as I stood up to leave, Eddie stood up with me and said, 'Oh, I know Mrs Featherstone, do you want me to show you the way?'

'Okay,' I replied, thinking I could use all the help I could get on those illogical country roads.

'You don't understand about the ducks do you?' Eddie asked me as we set off walking.

'I don't understand a lot of things around here,' I laughed, not worrying so much about it now, and hoping more than ever that I was on my way home.

18
Big Questions, Little Answers

Eddie did know the way to Mrs Featherstone's and he took me right to the door, even stopping to say hello as she answered it. Mrs Featherstone kindly invited me in for a second time, and we relived the moment of enjoying a cup of hot cocoa together before we started chatting about more serious matters. As I've said before, Mrs Featherstone seemed to be the only person who had really given the impression that she had been expecting me, and I knew this was my last chance to make some sense of the things that still had me confused. So as we sat there at her dining table I began my inquisition, which she was only too happy to comply with.

'Have you been to the lake?' was my first question as it was at the forefront of my mind.

'Oh yes, the lake is the most beautiful part of town,' Mrs Featherstone answered affectionately.

'But what is so special about the ducks?' I asked at last.

'Oh the ducks,' she laughed, 'they're lovely aren't they? Yes, they come here in the wintertime. It's never too cold for them here and they know how to crack the safe code off by heart. I guess it's easier when you can fly.'

How can such an unusual answer to such an unusual question make so much sense? I had obviously spent too much time there; it really was home time!

'Is it true then, that in order to be let out of here I had to feed the ducks?'

'Yes, it's true. It may seem a little cruel I know, but if you hadn't come across the lake by accident I would be sending you out looking for it now. The ducks are like our pets. We look after them and they keep coming back here. If they didn't the lake wouldn't have such an important purpose and might begin to die, and if it did it would close up our window to the sun.'

'So do all lakes have a purpose in life, the same as umbrellas and unfinished books?'

'Paddy, everything has a purpose. Everything was created by God with a purpose, or invented by man with a purpose, or else what would be the point?'

'Okay, I think I understand,' I said, although I'm not sure if I did. Things were invented for a reason, of course, or to solve a particular problem, but it didn't explain why the people of Tunnelton treated inanimate objects as if they were alive.

'Why is the town called Tunnelton?' I asked next, changing the subject and wondering why that question hadn't occurred to me before.

'Well, I'm sure you've heard of catacombs,' Mrs Featherstone explained. 'They are underground dwellings, some of which were man-made to serve as shelters during wars, some are underground graveyards that have existed for hundreds of thousands of years, and some, like this one have been created entirely by the Earth, bit by bit over time.'

'So does Tunnelton exist in a catacomb somewhere underground on planet Earth?'

'Well, not exactly,' she went on. 'This particular catacomb has existed for as long as planet Earth and it grew so big that when it reached the same length as planet Earth's diameter it had to break free.'

'So the Earth and Tunnelton separated? How?'

'Tunnelton shed its skin of Earth just like a snake. The Earth kept on spinning just like it always has, and the momentum of the separation has kept Tunnelton spinning alongside it ever since.'

'So they do literally run parallel to each other?'

'That's right,' she smiled.

'But surely Tunnelton can't be as big as you say? I've been round it in a week.'

'Oh it is dear, believe me, and it's still growing, becoming more of a sphere like the Earth, transforming itself into a planet I suppose, although we've always referred to it as a planet anyway. It's just that here we don't use up the whole of the surface for ourselves, we don't need it, and so, a bit like the sun, we save it. Ninety-five per cent of Tunnelton is made up of rainforests and seas. The parts you have visited are the only populated areas of the planet, and yes, you can see it all in a week, probably in a couple of days if you really try.'

'So how does all that explain the Daylight-Saving theory?'

'It's really quite simple Paddy,' Mrs Featherstone began again as she got up to make us some more cocoa. 'We share the same sun as planet Earth, but whereas it takes planet Earth twenty-four hours to rotate once on its axis, it only takes Tunnelton eighteen hours, but because we run to a twenty-four hour clock as is really the only sensible thing to do, the light and dark that we get do not really fit in with the normal cycle of a day.'

'But if Tunnelton spins alongside the Earth, isn't it more like the moon? And why can't it be detected from Earth?'

Mrs Featherstone sat down again, put a second cup of cocoa in front of me and patted my hand.

'You mustn't think of it like a moon, because it certainly is not like a moon. The Earth's moon orbits it once a month, and the reason it is visible from the Earth is that at any one time half of the moon is lit up by the sun. But it isn't inhabited and it doesn't rely on the sun for photosynthesis, so it is therefore a satellite of the Earth rather than a neighbouring planet. The reason we can't be seen from Earth is a little more complicated. Firstly we are a lot closer to the Earth than the moon, or any other planets for that matter. We are so close that to the naked eye we would simply appear as a reflection. You see Tunnelton spins alongside the Earth but in the opposite direction and on such an axis that, without exception, every second of every day, Tunnelton Lake is facing the sun and our equator, which runs around the exact centre of our great sea, is facing the Earth's South Pole.'

'But if the lake and therefore the surrounding populated areas of Tunnelton are always facing the sun why does it get dark at all?'

'Relative to the Earth and the moon we are still, because every inch of our sea is the same as the next, and we rotate on an axis that makes absolutely no difference whatsoever to the movements of the rest of the solar system, but because of this we also get a lot of eclipses. We get them from the Earth, we get them from the moon, from Venus and Mercury; we can even get them from falling meteorites, so our daylight is very hit-and-miss, and because we are a self-sufficient planet, always have been, we have our own ways of using this to our advantage, because we are able, unlike any other planet, to control our own skies, by the amount of sun that is let in through the trees surrounding Tunnelton lake, as I'm sure you've already discovered, this works very similarly to solar power.'

'Do you think Tunnelton will get discovered?' I asked,

feeling quite protective of it now, perhaps even a little jealous of Mrs Featherstone for being able to live there all the time.

'Well, we'll see,' Mrs Featherstone answered, not sounding in the slightest bit worried about the future of her planet. 'The South Pole is populated, but only by a very few people, and there they have come to expect a view of nothingness, endless space, and they are not wrong, it is just our endless space. So you see, from every other point on the planet we are in hiding. Early Greek philosophers believed that the Earth was at the centre of the universe and that the sun and the stars orbited it, then Copernicus proved them wrong in the fifteenth century to some extent claiming that the Earth and the rest of the planets orbited the sun; this is called a heliocentric theory, but who knows, maybe it's time for a whole new theory,' she laughed.

'How do you know so much?' I asked her. 'And how did you end up in Tunnelton?'

'I was born here,' she replied, 'the same as everyone else that you will have met on your journey. My ancestors would have been in hiding in the catacomb when it broke free; there were hundreds of people in it at the time, people from all over the world, and enough to populate a small town, this small town.'

'So that explains the different accents, and the different generations of families that are here?'

'That's right, and although the lives of our ancestors have all followed very different paths, we have eventually become a community of our own making, and English was the most common language spoken by the majority, it is as simple as that. No one here has ever lived anywhere else. I'm not that old Paddy' she laughed again.

This made me think of Alfred though. He must have lived on Earth if he knew my great-great-grandad like he said he did. Mrs Featherstone caught me deep in thought and, as before, read my thoughts out loud.

'You met Alfred didn't you?' she asked.

'Yes.'

'Don't mind him, he's harmless. A little difficult to understand, but harmless.'

'But how can he still be alive if he knew my great-great-grandad?'

'He isn't,' she said bluntly. 'He isn't alive. He's like the thinkers in the park, but his body is dead. He had an imagination on him that old man, and the brains to go with it. Those thoughts will go on forever, imagination doesn't die Paddy.'

'No, I think I've already been told that,' I nodded, 'but how can I see them, Alfred and the thinkers in the park, if they're not really there?'

Mrs Featherstone smiled and for once didn't answer me. I think I was supposed to go away and ponder that one. What did it matter anyway? People see ghosts all the time, so it wasn't any weirder than that!

'And how exactly did I get here?' I asked, hoping to get a fuller picture. 'I don't mean by cracking the safe code, I mean how did I make the jump between the planets?'

'Well I can't really tell you that,' Mrs Featherstone replied, looking down into her cup of cocoa, 'but you remember the thunderstorm don't you?'

'Yes.'

'Well that's like our inter-planetary transport. Fast as lightning!' she laughed.

'So why didn't the sun come out for me when I first arrived?' I asked her.

'Because you were still on the landing pad' Mrs Featherstone told me, 'we can't have you getting any ideas about trying to jump back over the wall, that would be dangerous. My house acts as the check-in point for visitors. Once you've passed here you are recognised as an official guest and therefore the sun works for you.'

This somehow seemed to make sense, or at least as much sense as anything else did. I didn't need to understand everything, so I moved on.

'So you've seen the umbrella graveyard? And the war museum? And Lost Property Headquarters? And the Iris Mennison kids?'

'Paddy,' she shook her head, 'oh Paddy, of course. I've seen everything.'

'And does it all make sense to you?'

'Well of course.'

Was this my chance to ask all my questions or my chance to shut up? I took it as my chance to ask one more question and then leave with my curiosity intact, because where would I be in the real world if it weren't for my imagination? Stuck in a dead-end job with no ambition? At least I had my over-active daydreaming mind to get me through the slightest boring, unfulfilled moment of my day. Understanding began to seem over-rated and I'd probably had my fair share of education, at its most pure, over the last week and maybe, just maybe, I should have learnt to recognise when it's time to quit. And this was it. And so, ladies and gentlemen, for my last question, I put it to you, Mrs Featherstone, 'How do I get home?'

'The way you came in dear, of course.'

Of course.

19

Time Warp

It was still only early afternoon when I left Mrs Featherstone's house and set out on my return journey. When I had first arrived in Tunnelton, having stumbled across Mrs Featherstone's doorstep, by fate if you wish to believe that, or just by accident, it was not only raining but also very dark due to the thunderstorm. Knowing that I had to find the way I came in was one thing, but actually finding it was quite another. Other than it being near to Mrs Featherstone's house, and that in itself I could only assume as I knew I didn't remember everything about my arrival, I didn't know where to start looking. After all, I hadn't seen the entrance to the town from this side the first time around, so how would I recognise it?

Mrs Featherstone had not so much said goodbye as just disappeared after our little reunion, out of the mysterious kitchen door again, leaving me to find my way without any further directions. I stepped off the front porch and, using the logic that any direction would be as good as the next I turned left and hoped for the best. This path (which didn't in fact lead me directly to the exit, but I'll explain that in a minute) at least allowed me to encounter one more Tunnelton character before I left for the real world. I had chosen the road to the left because it seemed to take me away from the roads that were familiar to me. I was walking in the opposite direction to the path I had taken on my way to Deer Mountain, and the surrounding fields were becoming more sparse the further I walked, until I found myself on a well-trodden dirt track free of farmhouses, stone walls and streetlights. The sun was still out but the darkness of the ground and the density of the surrounding trees made the atmosphere a little dank and eerie. I was watching my feet as I fought to keep my grip on the track as well as keeping my eye on the direction in which I was heading, and it was because of this, not because of my lack of observation (which you must know by now could not possibly be the case) that I didn't notice the huge black horse walking towards me. In fact, to tell you the truth, I didn't notice it until it was standing right in front of me; its enormous head with bulging eyes and flaring nostrils looking down over me. It made me jump and almost scream, but there was no need to be alarmed. The horse had stopped next to me and as I raised my hand to rub its nose, it shook itself and whinnied in a friendly kind of way, if that's possible! It was a beautiful, tall, well-groomed black horse with a shiny mane and a clean blue coat, but there was no one around, no one walking behind it or shouting its name from the next field. It didn't have a bridle on, so I assumed it wasn't meant to be led anywhere. Maybe this was just where it lived and it was having an afternoon stroll, much the same as me, although no doubt without so much confusion.

Rather than cause any unintentional conflict with this enormous animal twice the height of me and with no doubt hundreds of times the strength, I began to walk on past it, quietly but confidently whilst avoiding its back legs, as I learnt the hard way once before when I was young! But as I walked by, the horse whinnied again, this time a lot louder, and, when I turned around to face it, it seemed to beckon me with its head. Now, as unlikely as this may seem, in comparison to my previous few days it didn't stand out as anything particularly out of the ordinary to me! However, I stood still for a moment, a little unsure of what to do, and then the horse took a sharp right turn through a gap in the trees so I decided to take my chances and I followed it onto another, very similar dirt track running at ninety degrees to the one I had originally chosen, a track that took me, eventually, on a path that ran away from the back of Mrs Featherstone's house, which I could still just about make out in the distance.

I followed at a safe distance as the horse led me out of the woods and into a playing field. Now I knew where I was! This was the playing field behind the three shops in Hepby, the field I had stepped over the wall into in search of the light. The sun was now getting dimmer, which I hadn't experienced in Tunnelton before. Usually it appeared to be either on or off, without a sunrise or sunset in between, but now it was definitely fading as I strained my eyes to look for the familiar shops. I still couldn't see them, even when the horse led me right up to the wall itself, because over the other side, where there should have been the three shops with a path running behind them and through the gaps the main road with the lay-by, it was just pitch black. I turned, rather thoughtlessly, to the horse for some sort of clue, feeling quite defeated as I had literally drawn a dead-end. The horse though, unlike me, was not lost, and knew exactly what to do. It shouted out with an echoing, deafening roar, something that the skies obviously understood because on hearing this (as I had experienced after cracking the safe code), the sky opened up, let out a similar roar in reply, lit up the field, in fact the whole of Tunnelton, with a sweeping wave of white light, then to a crashing thunder closed up, taking everything in view away and leaving me shocked, soaking wet and all alone on the other side of the wall, on the path at the back of the DIY shop.

I must have been thrown over the wall with some force because I had ended up on the wet ground, my hands and knees covered in mud. I stood up and made some attempt at brushing myself off before following the path round onto the main road. I looked across the road to see my car there, just where I'd left it a week ago. I rushed to get in it and out of the storm. I rummaged around in my rucksack, which was still there on the back seat, for my mobile phone. I was surprised to find that there weren't any messages on it. Why hadn't people been wondering where I was? But it was just as I, almost panic-stricken, rang my parents' number that it all started to make sense. I looked at the clock in my car as my mother answered the phone; it was quarter past eight.

'Hello.'

'Hi mum, it's just me, I'm calling...'

'Missing us already are you?' she joked. 'Fiona and Mike are round from next door, you just missed them.'

'Oh.' I needed to ask some questions without her getting suspicious about my sanity. 'What date is it?' I tried to ask calmly, as if I was just being my usual disorganised self. 'Is it the twenty-eighth?'

'Yes, that's right,' she answered, and I could hear the frown in her voice. 'Why?'

'No, nothing, sorry, just getting a bit confused, just with Christmas. You know me, I don't know what day it is most of the time.'

'Oh, okay love, well drive carefully, and I hope tomorrow's okay back at work.'

I could tell now that she was itching to get back to her guests.

'Okay mum, bye.'

And with that I turned on the engine for a quick escape and the radio for additional date and time confirmation, which I got almost instantly. I set off on my way to York, having not missed a single day of my ordinary life, and having not been away for long enough to be missed. It was still the exact date and time that I had stepped out of the car. I hadn't missed the New Year's Eve celebrations after all!

20
Finish

So now you're wondering how I know it wasn't all just a dream. Well, I don't suppose I can actually prove it, but I know I was there, in Tunnelton, and I lived every one of my days there with my eyes wide open. When I look back on it, like now when I'm telling you the whole story of it, I feel a certain amount of pride at having been a part of that wonderful life, and honoured to have met all those care-free, humorous, interesting people and to have learnt so much from them.

I can never watch a sunset now without thinking of Daylight-Saving, or see someone in baggy black jeans without looking for the yellow stitching and the logo on the back pocket. I don't look at ducks with quite the same disregard any more and I certainly can't walk past an abandoned umbrella without wanting to pick it up and fix it!

Of course I haven't told anyone about it, well until now. I certainly wouldn't expect my regular, down-to-earth family to believe me, or understand its importance. I've brought back a few souvenirs with me: the Lost Property guide, the three of diamonds playing card, which now serves as my lucky charm, the war museum ticket and the rather unflattering Parkside Motel T-shirt! I'm not quite sure what happened to the clothes I borrowed from Mr and Mrs Stitch, I only know that when I landed back in Hepby I was wearing my own clothes, the ones I set off in, so I'm guessing they got them back somehow, and I got back my own screensaver!

I think about Mrs Featherstone sometimes, Stephanie and

René, Mr Adams and Rupert, Lorrie, Mr and Mrs Stitch and Sebastian, Dorian of course, and Alfred, Neville and Tobias, Claris and Clarence, Eddie, the mountain-climbers, the Iris Mennison kids, the speakers in the park, the librarian, the vicar and, of course, the horse that had a much better sense of direction than me and led me out of there!

It was an experience! That's the least credit I can give it. But it was much more than that, and although it's been nice to share my story with you, it's very difficult to really tell it like it is. Maybe, if you happen to find yourself in Hepby one rainy winter's night, you might pull into the lay-by across from the DIY shop and, on the off-chance that there's a single swaying white light lurking behind it, you might take a little walk around the shops, twice anti-clockwise then once clockwise. And don't forget to feed the ducks!